life

afterlife

*Join*

*with*

*Gold*

**UpSet Press**

PO Box 200340
Brooklyn, NY 11220

upsetpress.org

Afterwards: Join with Gold

Copyright © 2025 by Robert Booras

All poems/scenes written by Robert Booras

All characters, poems, scenes (setting and dialogue) are fictitious (wildly imagined by the author). Any likeness to real events or people, living or not, including those with the same name, is coincidental.

All rights reserved. No part of this book may be used or reproduced in any form or by any means without the written permission of the author, except in the case of brief quotations embodied in critical articles or reviews. Requests for permission to use or reproduce text from this book should be addressed in writing to publisher.

—

All playlists created by Robert Booras
However, these can be recreated, altered, augmented, as desired...

All French text by Antonin Artaud from *artandpopularculture.com*, *Artaud The Mômo* (Diaphanes, 2020), and *Les Tarahumaras* (L'ARBALÈTE) EXCEPT French text in "Noise of Sosúa," whch is by author.

UpSet Press is an independent, not-for-profit (501c3 tax exempt) organization advancing thought-provoking works of literature, including translated works, to promote curiosity, dialogue, growth, i.e., to upset the status quo.

—

ISBN 978-1-937357-05-4
Library of Congress Control Number: 2025931239
Printed in US
First Edition [Title Cards Version]

—

Book and cover design by
Jessica D'Elena-Tweed

# Contents (1,024 songs)

Characters     8
Glossary     10

## ¹*Interludes' Playlists Corona #3* (Posthumous)     11

Secret to Life     12
    (Memories) [Time + Space]     13
    (Memories) [Time]     14
    (Selene) [Hold You Again]     15
    (Πάθος) [Αθήνα]     16
    (Inner Voice) [Deep Forest Green]     17
    (God) [Knows I Tried]     18
    (Astronaut) [Andata]     19
    (Sosúa) [Tu Ta To]     20
    (Selene) [Ain't Gonna Call]     21
    (Polyglossia) [Don't Die]     22
    (Self-Hate) [Beast in Me]     23
    (Heart Nebula) [Galaxies]     24
    (Kintsugi) [Instrumental]     25
    (Addiction) [Cocaine]     26
    (Insomnia) [Without You]     27
    (Adonis) [Captain Save A Hoe]     28
    (Fucking) [Bite the Pillow]     29
    (Selene) [Heavy Dirty Soul]     30
    (Defeat) [Going Home]     31
    (Hate) [Cherry]     32
    (Voodoo Pussy) [Rump Punch]     33
    (Road Trip) [Nightdrive with You]     34
    (Beyond Green) [Into the Freedom]     35
    (Selene) [Forget]     36
    (Soul Nebula) [Wait]     37
    (Devil) [Take Me]     38
    (Acid Trip) [Lay Back]     39
    (Kink) [Poly]     40
    (Heart in a Box) [Anything You Want]     41
    (FFFado) [Lisbon]     42
    (Kintsugi) [Aftercare]     43

Reading Between Lines — 44

# ²*Afterlife* *(Beyond Love)* — 45

| | |
|---|---|
| PACMAN NEBULA | 47 |
| My Afflictions / My Menace (My Altar) | 49 |
| (Scenes & Poems) Of GOEW | 52 |
| WIZARD NEBULA | 53 |
| Afterlife | 55 |
| CHAMPAGNE ROOM | 57 |
| Three Guys Walk into A Bar | 59 |
| Guide to Trap a Gringo | 60 |
| BARTENDER | 61 |
| No Swimming | 63 |
| OSCAR ACCEPTANCE SPEECH | 65 |
| Shark (Baby) vs. Bear (Daddy) | 67 |
| THE NEXT MORNING | 69 |

# ³*Aftermath* *(Hereafter)* — 73

| | |
|---|---|
| (Paradox) Of Love | 74 |
| IMPROMPTU EULOGY (GOD'S SKIT) | 75 |
| An Explanation of Truth | 77 |
| CACA | 79 |
| Bona Fide Witch | 80 |
| POST SCRIPTUM | 81 |
| Cold Plunge | 83 |
| CAT'S EYE NEBULA | 87 |
| Little by Little | 89 |
| Side by Side | 90 |
| AFTER SPICER (A SÉANCE) | 91 |
| An Embodied Experience | 95 |
| Rhizome (Ballad of Escape) | 96 |

## ⁴Noise of Sosúa *(Tinnitus)* — 97

| | |
|---|---|
| Balcony | 98 |
| A GREAT CRY | 99 |
| (Barking) | 101 |
| (Dying) | 102 |
| HAPPY VALENTINE'S DAY XOXOXO | 103 |
| Of Spiders | 107 |
| Lost and Found (Art of Self-Portraiture) | 108 |
| FANTASTICAL LIARS | 109 |
| An Opera (Pyre) | 111 |
| Desperation in Adonis | 112 |
| ALONE IN CHANTY'S APARTMENT | 113 |
| Playa Alicia (Reprise) | 115 |
| Going Home | 116 |

## ⁵Aerodrome *(Passport Control)* — 117

| | |
|---|---|
| Aerodrome (Arrival) | 118 |
| A REAL TRAGEDY | 119 |
| Myth of the Two Brothers | 121 |
| THREE GUYS WALK INTO A BAR (SCENE) | 123 |
| Chanty Dolarz | 124 |

| | |
|---|---|
| Complete Playlist of *Afterwards…* | 125 |
| Black Magic Does Exist (Departure) | 128 |

# Characters

*Mute the Noise | Wiley*

In fiction
They use ornate language

In courthouses
They use legalese
Circular
Not even lawyers can decipher

In the news
They use propaganda

No wonder in real life
We shield ourselves from words

(P.S. Study behavior)

L'intelligence est venue après la sottise,
laquelle l'a toujours sodomisée de près,—
ET APRÈS.

Ce qui donne une idée de
l'infini trajet.

—Antonin Artaud, *"L'EXÉCRATION DU PÈRE-MÈRE"*

# Glossary

| | | | | | |
|---|---|---|---|---|---|
| **Gil Scott-Heron** | sex work | *afterlife* | nightlife |
| | cheetah cage | *apartment* | strip club |
| | Monsieur | *Antonin Artaud* | Mômo |
| | genitalia | *CACA* | fornication |
| **Explanations** | NGC 6543 | *Cat's Eye Nebula* | Caldwell 6 |
| | streetwalker | *cheetah* | siren |
| | afterlife | *control* | fiction |
| | retreat | *home* | base |
| | cum (v.) | *leche* | semen |
| | movie | *life* | marriage |
| | ebullience | *love* | chaos |
| | NGC 281 | *Pacman Nebula* | Sh2-184 |
| | side lovers | *stars* | daddies |
| | NGC 7380 | *Wizard Nebula* | Sh2-142 |

New Characters:    Antonin Artaud
                            Chanty Dolarz

**MONSIEUR:** c'étaient des mots
inventés pour définir des choses
qui existaient
ou n'existaient pas
en face de
l'urgence pressante
d'un besoin:
celui de supprimer l'idée,
l'idée et son mythe,

(P.S. This glossary is offered as amulet)

*Infinity* | The xx

# 3 INTERLUDES' PLAYLISTS CORONA

*(Posthumous)*

**MÔMO:**

tu n'es plus là
mais rien ne te quitte,
tu as tout conservé
sauf toi-même

et que t'importe puisque
le monde
est là.

# Secret to **Life**

*The Gambler | Kenny Rogers*

*Money* and *Active Listening*
First off, you need money to do what you want
And to persuade others
Then, active listening

Everyone wants to be heard
More than they want to be seen
Everyone wants to be a star
In their own movie called *Life*

When you get someone talking
They become an actor
Giving a monologue
And you become the producer

Who has more control of the narrative?
The actor or the producer?

(P.S. The bewitched man is at last cast)

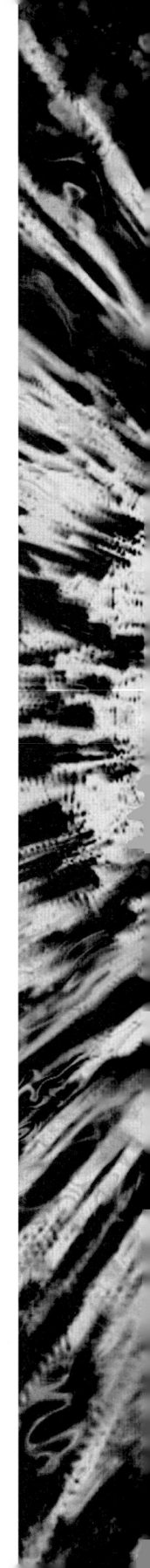

# (Memories) [Time+Space]

| | | |
|---|---|---|
| Blue Side (Outro) | j-hope | 1:31 |
| Sex To Me | Charlotte Cardin | 3:36 |
| Two Weeks | Grizzly Bear | 4:06 |
| Memories | Eden Prince, Nonô | 2:29 |
| Moving Through Water | Marta, Tricky | 1:53 |
| Heaven's Only Wishful | MorMor | 4:03 |
| Are You Still a Lover | Sassy 009 | 3:39 |
| Doing It To Death | The Kills | 4:08 |
| Better Now | Post Malone | 3:51 |
| All Alone | Gorillaz, Martina Topley-Bird, Roots Manuva | 3:33 |
| No One Noticed | The Marias | 3:57 |
| Berlin Lovers | Still Corners | 2:38 |
| Lucifer, My Love | Twin Temple | 5:49 |
| Always See Your Face | Love | 3:29 |
| Two Weeks | FKA twigs | 4:08 |
| So Good at Being in Trouble | Unknown Mortal Orchestra | 3:50 |
| Road Head | Japanese Breakfast | 3:15 |
| Sharks | Imagine Dragons | 3:11 |
| Sex, Drugs, Etc. | Beach Weather | 3:17 |
| I Don't Know You | Mannequin Pussy | 3:44 |
| TIL FURTHER NOTICE | Travis Scott, James Blake, 21 Savage | 5:15 |
| Astronaut | Griff | 3:35 |
| HUMBLE. | Kendrick Lamar | 2:57 |
| Pussy That Blows Your Mind | Angie, Harrison First | 3:37 |
| Genesis | Spencer. | 4:29 |
| I Come With Knives | IAMX | 4:23 |
| **Time + Space** | **Thievery Corporation, Lou Lou Ghelickhani** | **4:33** |
| Who Taught You How to Love | King Dude | 5:23 |
| Fountains | Drake, Tems | 3:12 |
| Where Damage Isn't Already Done | The Radio Dept. | 2:44 |
| Destroy Myself Just For You | Montell Fish | 2:26 |

1hr 52m

# (Memories) [Time]

| | | |
|---|---|---|
| You Know What I Mean | Cults | 2:30 |
| Sex God | The Brand New Heavies | 4:54 |
| The Book of Love | The Magnetic Fields | 2:42 |
| Memories | David Guetta, Kid Cudi | 3:30 |
| All Night | The Endorphins, Joe Lefty | 3:58 |
| If Only | The Marias | 2:36 |
| (The Death of Ruby) | Ruby Haunt | 1:42 |
| Indestructible | Robyn | 3:41 |
| Self Love | Jayson Lyric, Nevaeh | 2:39 |
| Si un jour | La Femme | 2:38 |
| Let Your Love Light Shine | Ann Peebles | 3:59 |
| Falling | Alesso | 3:22 |
| One Of A Kind Love Affair | Kadhja Bonet | 4:38 |
| Smooth Criminal | Michael Jackson | 4:18 |
| Keep Lying | Donna Missal | 3:36 |
| Sasha | Siki Daha | 3:17 |
| Love on You | Dizzy Fae | 3:10 |
| Come On Let's Go | Broadcast | 3:17 |
| Big World 4 Lovers | BEA1991 | 3:53 |
| Gemini Moon | Reneé Rapp | 2:41 |
| Look At My Body Pt. II | Mabel, Shygirl | 2:40 |
| 25th Floor | Patti Smith | 4:04 |
| Truth Hurts | Lizzo | 2:53 |
| Oh, Round Lake | Novo Amor | 2:55 |
| Deeper Than Love | Colleen Green | 6:06 |
| Kiss of fire | WOODZ | 3:16 |
| **Time Will Tell** | **Blood Orange** | **5:39** |
| To Be Loved | SEV, Brika | 3:53 |
| Marigold | Jelani Aryeh | 4:05 |
| Too Soon | The Radio Dept. | 1:18 |
| I Want You | Mitski | 3:04 |

**1hr 46m**

# (Selene) [Hold You Again]

| | | |
|---|---|---|
| Season of the Witch | Donovan | 4:54 |
| ...Baby one more time | The Marias | 2:05 |
| Careless Whisper | George Michael | 5:00 |
| Retrograde | James Blake | 3:44 |
| Memories | Maroon 5 | 3:09 |
| Karma | Sarah Kinsley | 3:58 |
| Talia | King Princess | 3:28 |
| Break My Love | RÜFÜS DU SOL | 4:20 |
| Without You | David Guetta, Usher | 3:28 |
| Mi Querido Amor | Stevie Wonder | 2:53 |
| She's My Witch | Kip Tyler | 2:22 |
| Falling | LÉON | 3:53 |
| Saturn | Sleeping At Last | 4:50 |
| Walkin' After Midnight | Ki:Theory, Maura Davis | 3:12 |
| Take Care | Beach House | 5:48 |
| Lovefool | The Cardigans | 3:14 |
| Call me when ur lonely | Alaina Castillo | 2:40 |
| Swim Good | Frank Ocean | 4:17 |
| Monody | TheFatRat, Laura Brehm | 4:50 |
| All I Ever Asked | Rachel Chinouriri | 3:38 |
| Dancer in the Dark | Scratch Massive, Maud Geffray | 4:32 |
| Future Starts Slow | The Kills | 4:08 |
| Over Again | Sir Chloe | 2:42 |
| Flower face – Angela (I dream of you softly) | eevee | 1:30 |
| Moon | Reneé Rapp | 3:00 |
| Hometown | Twenty One Pilots | 3:55 |
| **Hold you again** | **The Millenial Club** | **3:55** |
| Deamon Lover | Shocking Blue | 6:05 |
| What Once Was | Her's | 4:15 |
| I'm a Fool to Want You | Billie Holiday | 3:23 |
| I Know You | Faye Webster | 4:12 |

1hr 57m

# (Πάθος) [Αθήνα]

| | | |
|---|---|---|
| Ώρα Να Γυρίσεις | Μαλού | 3:46 |
| Αχ Κορίτσι Μου | Γιάννης Πλούταρχος | 3:53 |
| Ελπίδα | Κωνσταντίνος Αργυρός | 4:04 |
| Έτσι Αγαπάω Εγώ | Στέλιος Ρόκκος | 4:49 |
| Να Είσαι Εκεί | Μιχάλης Χατζηγιάννης | 4:18 |
| Βενζινάδικο | Άλκηστις Πρωτοψάλτη | 3:14 |
| Μάτια Μου | Αλέξια | 3:52 |
| Πες Του – DJ Pantelis & Vasilis Koutonias Remix | Zan Batist, DJ Pantelis, Vasilis Koutonias | 4:07 |
| Μίλα Μου | Κώστας Καραφώτης, Μάρω Λύτρα | 3:46 |
| PASSIONE | Fred De Palma | 2:43 |
| Εγώ Σ' Αγάπησα Εδω | Ελένη Τσαλιγοπούλου | 3:39 |
| Το Tango της Νεφέλης | Χάρις Αλεξίου | 4:07 |
| Ελένη | Άννα Βίσση | 4:56 |
| Σε θέλω σαν Τρελός - Live | Σάκης Ρουβάς | 4:21 |
| Σε θέλω, Με θέλεις | Άννα Βίσση, Σάκης Ρουβάς | 4:34 |
| Αγάπη Μου | Γιώργος Παπαδόπουλος | 3:21 |
| Δεν Είσαι Εσύ | Χρίστος Αντωνιάδης | 3:34 |
| Τι ήμουνα για 'σένα | Αντώνης Ρέμος | 3:07 |
| Σώμα Μου | Νότης Σφακιανάκης | 3:46 |
| Ξημερώματα | Κωνσταντίνος Αργυρός | 3:01 |
| Είχα κάποτε μια Αγάπη | Παντελής Παντελίδης | 4:35 |
| Αν είσαι ένα Αστέρι | Νίκος Βέρτης | 4:35 |
| Όλα Λάθος | Έλλη Κοκκίνου | 3:24 |
| Όλα Σε Θυμίζουν | Χάρις Αλεξίου | 3:52 |
| Πες Μου Μια Λέξη | Μάρω Κοντού, Γιάννης Μπέζος | 2:50 |
| Η Επιμονή Σου | Ελεωνόρα Ζουγανέλη, Κώστας Λειβαδάς | 4:01 |
| **Αθήνα Μου** | **Κωνσταντίνος Αργυρός** | **3:49** |
| Αν Είσαι η Αγάπη | Γιάννης Πλούταρχος | 3:39 |
| Ένα Γράμμα | Νότης Σφακιανάκης | 4:51 |
| Ένα Φιλί | Χάρις Αλεξίου | 4:10 |
| Χιλιόμετρα | APON | 2:38 |

2hr

# (Inner Voice) [Deep Forest Green]

| | | |
|---|---|---|
| *Advice to young girls* | Inga Copeland, Actress | 4:48 |
| *FUNKENTOLOGY* | BLK ODYSSY | 2:53 |
| *Final Form* | Pearly Drops | 2:57 |
| *Teeth* | Mallrat | 3:09 |
| *Moon Diagrams* | Moon Diagrams | 3:40 |
| *Odyssey* | Yndi, Dream Koala | 6:10 |
| *The Whole Point of No Return* | Robert Wyatt | 1:26 |
| *Vibrate* | Drug Store Romeos | 2:35 |
| *Outro/Honest* | Quelle Chris, Chris Keys, Marcella Arguello | 4:44 |
| *Death of the Phone Call* | Whatever, Dad | 1:35 |
| *Fool* | Frankie Cosmos | 2:04 |
| *From the Air* | Laurie Anderson | 4:33 |
| *Also Sprach Zarathustra* | Deodato | 9:01 |
| *Wet Dream* | Wet Leg | 2:20 |
| *Sweetest Fruit* | St. Vincent | 3:55 |
| *Love's Boy* | Sol Seppy | 3:47 |
| *Climbing My Dark Hair* | Elysian Fields | 3:30 |
| *Sea, Swallow Me* | Cocteau Twins, Harold Budd | 3:09 |
| *Bring Down the Birds – Outtake* | Herbie Hancock | 1:46 |
| *I'm Sorry We Lied* | Blood Orange | 4:00 |
| *It Almost Worked* | TV Girl | 2:32 |
| *Airborne Ashes* | Eartheater, Aleksandir | 4:29 |
| *A Bird's Last Look* | Macabre Plaza | 1:10 |
| *Welcome and goodbye* | Dream, Ivory | 2:21 |
| *Witchking / Angmar* | E L L E | 3:06 |
| *The Moth & The Flame* | Les Deux Love Orchestra | 3:56 |
| *Deep Forest Green* | Husky Rescue | 3:59 |
| *Love Is Loving – Photay Remix* | Scrimshire, Faye Houston, Omar, Photay | 3:25 |
| *Sky Saw* | Brian Eno | 3:28 |
| *French Kiss* | Still Corners | 4:32 |
| *I See You Baby* | Haiku Hands | 3:16 |

**1hr 48m**

# (God) [Knows I Tried]

| | | |
|---|---|---|
| ...And the Gods Made Love | Jimi Hendrix | 1:23 |
| All Along the Watchtower | Jimi Hendrix | 4:01 |
| Follow God | Kanye West | 1:45 |
| THIS YEAR (Blessings) | Victor Thompson, Ehis 'D' Greatest | 2:06 |
| Oh My God | A Tribe Called Quest, Busta Rhymes | 3:29 |
| God's Gonna Cut You Down | Dead Posey | 2:26 |
| To Know Him Is To Love Him – Live | Amy Winehouse | 2:25 |
| The Devil Went Down to Georgia | The Charlie Daniels Band | 3:35 |
| Chase The Devil | Max Romeo, The Upsetters | 3:26 |
| Asiwaju | Ruger | 3:36 |
| God Complex | VIOLENT VIRA | 2:59 |
| THANK GOD | Travis Scott | 3:05 |
| The Man Who Sold The World – Live | Nirvana | 4:21 |
| On GOD | Mustard, YG, Tyga, A$AP Ferg, A$AP Rocky | 4:23 |
| Devil's Advocate | The Neighbourhood | 3:06 |
| I'm God | Clams Casino, Imogen Heap | 4:38 |
| GUD | Zae France | 2:46 |
| Way Down In The Hole | Tom Waits | 3:30 |
| Pick Myself Up – Live | Peter Tosh | 4:47 |
| Lord Knows Best | Dirty Beaches | 3:24 |
| Devil Devil | MILCK | 4:19 |
| Science/Visions | CHVRCHES | 3:58 |
| I Shall Be Released – Live at Sin-é | Jeff Buckley | 5:21 |
| Godspeed | Frank Ocean | 2:58 |
| Don't Let Problems Get You Down | Horace Andy | 2:50 |
| All For Us | Labrinth, Zendaya | 3:12 |
| God Knows I Tried | Lana Del Rey | 4:41 |
| Lovely Day | Bill Withers | 4:15 |
| God Said No | Dan Bern | 5:31 |
| Oh My God | Michael Franti & Spearhead | 5:08 |
| Flying Into the Sun | Crystal Stilts | 3:34 |

1hr 50m

# (Astronaut) [Andata]

| | | |
|---|---|---|
| Greenland | Emancipator | 3:11 |
| Tommib | System Olympia | 1:38 |
| The Lost Page (From Judee's Journal) | Judee Sill, David Allred | 1:41 |
| Geometría del Universo | Colleen | 2:50 |
| 茜空 (Akanesora) | Ironomi, Reiko Imanishi | 9:55 |
| 'Long As You Know You're Living Yours | Keith Jarrett, Jan Garbarek, Palle Danielsson, Jon Christensen | 6:11 |
| Agape | Dead Can Dance | 6:54 |
| The E and D Blues (E for Ella and D for Duke) | Ella Fitzgerald, Duke Ellington | 4:48 |
| Yearning to this music | Ronald Langestraat | 2:18 |
| Naweye toro | Ali Farka Touré, Toumani Diabaté | 4:22 |
| Excitement (Three Moods) | Sven Libaek | 1:03 |
| Falling | 3LAU, DNMO | 3:29 |
| Lacrimosa | Wolfgang Amadeus Mozart, Lisa Beckley, Elena Filipova, et al. | 3:25 |
| Song on the Beach | Arcade Fire, Owen Pallett | 3:36 |
| ハピネス (Happines Is Me and You) | Shigeo Sekito | 4:15 |
| Windswept – Reprise | Johnny Jewel | 3:54 |
| Boardwalk Dulce | Emancipator, Asher Fulero, Dab Records | 1:38 |
| Ocean Floors | Headphone Activist | 3:52 |
| Beyond Love | Iván Torrent, Lara Ausensi | 4:14 |
| The Untold | Secession Studios | 3:12 |
| Girls in Pearls | S.Maharba | 1:17 |
| Clouds Up | Air | 1:31 |
| Captain Of None | Colleen | 5:57 |
| Só | Hareton Salvanini | 3:13 |
| Moon | Little People | 3:48 |
| Menace | Rezz | 3:16 |
| **Andata** | **Ryuichi Sakamoto** | **2:53** |
| Peace and Love Dub | Augustus Pablo | 2:52 |
| The Poetry of Earth (Geophony) | Max Richter | 3:58 |
| Just Give Me One More Day | Alejandro Vargas, Alej | 2:11 |
| A Gentle Dissolve | Thievery Corporation | 2:50 |

1hr 50m

# (Sosúa) [Tu Ta To]

| | | |
|---|---|---|
| Grima Remix | Zenemij, Dowel King, Lymm.19 | 3:13 |
| Seco | NTG, Chocoleyrol | 2:45 |
| BBY BOO – REMIX | iZaak, JHAYCO, Anuel AA | 4:35 |
| CHAPA | Yailin la Mas Viral, Puyalo Pantera | 2:00 |
| Dale 2 | Yailin la Mas Viral, Kreizy k | 2:28 |
| WYA REMIX RED | J Abdiel, De La Rose, Yan Block, iZaak, Jay Wheeler | 5:21 |
| Del Kilo | Anuell AA, Treintisiete, Yailin la Mas Viral | 3:46 |
| Rapido | Amenazzy, Farruko, Myke Towers, Rochy RD | 2:33 |
| Boomerang | Romeo Santos | 4:07 |
| Quien Dijo | Yaisel LM, Hansel El De La H | 2:04 |
| Que La Choque | Rochy RD | 2:05 |
| Cierra La Puerta | Braulio Fogon, NTG | 2:09 |
| History | Luis Brown | 2:28 |
| No Te Quites | D'Flow Aka La Maldad | 2:01 |
| Si Antes Te Hubiera Conocido | KAROL G | 3:15 |
| El Malo | Aventura | 3:58 |
| Cuando Prendo | Rochy RD, Donaty | 2:40 |
| Mar | Romeo Santos | 3:23 |
| Le Doy | El Sicokario 42 | 2:10 |
| Bo Bo Bo | Jey One | 1:34 |
| Llame Pa Verte | Yaisel LM, Big Chriss & Draco Deville | 2:58 |
| TU TA TO | El Mello 06, Marino El Abusador | 2:08 |
| Boy Boy | Yaisel LM, Hansel El De La H | 2:14 |
| LA PRIMERA VEZ | Myke Towers, NTG | 2:51 |
| Oh Oh | Sensato, Shadow Blow | 3:23 |
| Chivirika | El Villanord, Yailin la Mas Viral | 3:30 |
| **Tu dice que tu ta to** | **Ezzy R, Yoan Retro** | **1:51** |
| AMARGURA | KAROL G | 2:50 |
| Pila De Nota | Bigoblin, JeycitoLM | 2:18 |
| Que linda | Lomiiel, Donaty, Papera, Leo RD | 2:17 |
| Mirame | Boy Wonder CF, Tivi Gunz, Nino Freestyle, Three Seven Music, The Chosen Few | 2:22 |

**1hr 27m**

# (Selene) [Ain't Gonna Call]

| | | |
|---|---|---|
| Season Of The Witch | Lana Del Rey | 4:07 |
| Crazy Sexy Dream Girl | Lolo Zouaï | 2:27 |
| Poison Heart | Depeche Mode | 3:17 |
| FIGURES | Jessie Reyez | 4:01 |
| Luna | Fear of Men | 3:53 |
| Too Late to Love You | Junebug, Ben Babbitt | 5:58 |
| Dead to Me | Maximum Love | 3:06 |
| Hurts Like Hell | Madison Beer, Offset | 3:27 |
| Re (Visit) | Fee Lion | 5:16 |
| Paranoid | Kanye West, Mr Hudson | 4:38 |
| Bringin' On The Heartbreak | Def Leppard | 4:34 |
| Motion Sickness | Phoebe Bridgers | 3:50 |
| GEMINI | BLK ODYSSY, Jackie Giroux | 2:38 |
| Cold as Ice | Foreigner | 3:23 |
| I've Had Enough | Melina KB | 3:31 |
| Heartless | The Weeknd | 3:18 |
| Bad idea! | girl in red | 3:40 |
| Barracuda | Heart | 4:22 |
| I Was A Fool | Sunflower Bean | 3:33 |
| SAME MISTAKE | DESTIN CONRAD, Alex Isley | 2:59 |
| Dancer in the Dark | Chase Atlantic | 4:12 |
| We're Just Making It Worse | Cameron Avery, Alexandra Savior | 4:04 |
| Inamorata | Mareux | 3:13 |
| Only Memories Remain | My Morning Jacket | 7:10 |
| X | Chris Brown | 4:21 |
| Voodoo | Godsmack | 4:43 |
| **Ain't Gonna Call** | **Yellow House** | **3:39** |
| L-Over | U.S. Girls | 4:06 |
| Cuntradiction | Lolahol | 3:47 |
| Memories | Conan Gray | 4:09 |
| Let It Die | Feist | 2:55 |

**2hr 2m**

# (Polyglossia) [Don't Die]

| | | |
|---|---|---|
| MAGICIAN | Lexie Liu | 3:33 |
| Tonight | Ghost Killer Track, D-Block Europe, OBOY | 3:35 |
| Til (*****) | Sassy 009 | 2:34 |
| Moonlight | Kali Uchis | 3:08 |
| Memories – Remix | Sigag Lauren, Ayra Starr | 3:01 |
| Outside (100 MPH) | Meek Mill | 3:19 |
| Séance | Chasu | 3:51 |
| Makeba – Dirty Ridin' Remix | Jain | 4:04 |
| I'm Doing Fine | J-BEATZ | 5:12 |
| Parisian Time | Desire, Jimmy Whoo | 3:34 |
| Couleur menthe à l'eau | Isaac Delusion | 3:32 |
| HIGH | CRO, Claudia Valentina | 2:48 |
| I'm Your Empress Of | Empress Of | 1:46 |
| Mamushi | Megan Thee Stallion, Yuki Chiba | 2:37 |
| Échame La Culpa | Luis Fonsi, Demi Lovato | 2:54 |
| Sexy Boy | Air | 4:58 |
| Liquid Smooth | Mitski | 2:50 |
| Mariana Trench | Dwara, Khotton | 4:23 |
| Life's Gone Down Low | The Lijadu Sisters | 4:57 |
| ¿QUIÉN TE MANDA? | Tei Shi | 3:39 |
| Favorite | Isabel LaRosa | 2:14 |
| SAOKO | ROSALÍA | 2:18 |
| A Guide For I & I | Thievery Corporation | 3:58 |
| Spell | Fireboy DML, Wande Coal | 2:53 |
| You Can't Kill Me I'm Alive | MeLoveMeAlot, KÅIKÅI, Mlma | 3:11 |
| Klefi | Hatari, Bashar Murad | 3:54 |
| **Stirb nicht vor mir (Don't Die Before I Do)** | **Rammstein** | **4:05** |
| LOVE BOMB | fromis_9 | 3:20 |
| One On One | The Knocks, Sofi Tukker | 3:32 |
| Así Así | Joalin | 2:56 |
| Karma | Mahmood, Woodkid | 3:34 |

**1hr 46m**

# (Self-Hate) [Beast in Me]

| | | |
|---|---|---|
| Total Depravity | The Veils | 4:07 |
| Invisible Fence | binki | 2:27 |
| Mercury | Steve Lacy | 3:17 |
| Made in Hell | Sara Laia | 4:01 |
| Bad Things | Cults | 3:53 |
| Been a Bad Woman | Black Casino and the Ghost | 5:58 |
| When You Die | MGMT | 3:06 |
| Cocoon | 070 Shake | 3:27 |
| I Can't Handle Change | Roar | 5:16 |
| Tenía Razón | Daniela Lalita | 4:38 |
| Freaks | Surf Curse | 4:34 |
| Falling Apart | Slow Pulp | 3:50 |
| All-American Bitch | Olivia Rodrigo | 2:38 |
| Steal My Sunshine | Portugal. The Man, Cherry Glazerr | 3:23 |
| Icing on the Cake | Grace Ives | 3:31 |
| Pretty Waste | BONES UK | 3:18 |
| Menace | Sheff G, Sleepy Hallow, Mozzy | 3:40 |
| Sharks | Bootleg Rascal | 4:22 |
| Party Poison | My Chemical Romance | 3:33 |
| BONDAGE | Fae | 2:59 |
| FREAK | Shygirl | 4:12 |
| Gasoline | Halsey | 4:04 |
| Are You Looking Up | Mk.gee | 3:13 |
| Angry | Mars Argo | 7:10 |
| The Gaping Mouth | Lowertown | 4:21 |
| DARKSIDE | Neoni | 4:43 |
| The Beast In Me | Johnny Cash | 3:39 |
| Love | BUNT., Johan Lenox | 4:06 |
| Boxed In | Sneaks | 3:47 |
| Stargirl | Salvia | 4:09 |
| I See You | The Horrors | 2:55 |

**1hr 45m**

# (Heart Nebula) [Galaxies]

| | | |
|---|---|---|
| Kalam | Mashrou' Leila | 4:06 |
| Vanilla | GACKT | 4:10 |
| Black Nirvana | Elodie | 3:04 |
| 靈 (Soul) | LAY | 2:59 |
| KINTSUGI | HUMBE | 3:58 |
| Tu Zaroori | Shaarib Toshi, Sunidhi Chauhan, Sharib Sabri | 4:50 |
| Αγάπη μου (Φαίδρα) | Μελίνα Μερκούρη | 3:32 |
| Paradinha | Anitta | 2:21 |
| Paraíso | Lucas Lucco, Pabllo Vittar | 2:43 |
| Fever | Soundz, FAVE | 3:06 |
| Divine créature | La Femme | 5:08 |
| 情人 (Lover) | KUN | 3:15 |
| Sungba – Remix | Asake, Burna Boy | 3:30 |
| Güllerin İçinden | MFÖ | 3:56 |
| Si No Me Falla El Corazon | Los Diablitos | 4:54 |
| Será que é amor – Ao vivo | Arlindo Cruz | 4:34 |
| Aaj Phir | Arijit Singh, Samira Koppikar | 4:22 |
| Γιατί Έχω Εσένα | Γιάννης Πλούταρχος | 3:15 |
| Ai Du | Ali Farka Touré, Ry Cooder | 7:10 |
| Zamilou | Bu Kolthoum | 2:22 |
| SHAKE AH | Tyla, Tony Duardo, Optimist Music ZA, Ez Maestro | 5:49 |
| Bebe | JIGGO, Ardian Bujupi | 3:28 |
| Baby | Gal Costa, Caetano Veloso | 3:33 |
| Dream Love | ICE杨长青 | 2:50 |
| Le soleil de ma vie | Sacha Distel, Brigitte Bardot | 3:07 |
| Στο Σκοτάδι – In the Darkness | Selofan | 3:16 |
| **Galassie** | **Irama** | **3:40** |
| Amour | Ya Levis | 3:04 |
| Corazón de Poeta | Jeanette | 4:33 |
| Kiss My Lips | BoA | 3:46 |
| Ayonha | Hamid Al Shaeri | 3:40 |

1hr 58m

# (Kintsugi) [Instrumental]

| | | |
|---|---|---|
| Awaken | Big Wild | 3:03 |
| Sex | Slugabed | 3:54 |
| Kintsugi | M/O/O/N | 4:06 |
| Ebullient | Floral | 5:20 |
| Lavender | BADBADNOTGOOD, KAYTRANADA | 3:20 |
| Birth4000 | Floating Points | 4:46 |
| High Tide | Brothertiger | 6:26 |
| Montserrat | Orquesta Del Plata | 5:10 |
| Reset | Gesaffelstein | 3:25 |
| The Hong Kong Triad | Thievery Corporation | 3:02 |
| The Golden Morning Breaks | Colleen | 5:23 |
| The Mercy of the Wind | Million Eyes | 1:46 |
| Low Tide of the Night | Everything But The Girl | 4:45 |
| The Phoenix | Lindsey Stirling | 4:05 |
| Because This Must Be | Nils Frahm | 2:46 |
| Charlie | Paul Sabin | 1:53 |
| Flare | RAIZHELL | 2:24 |
| Wind Surf Ballad | Dominique Guiot | 2:26 |
| High Tide – Doss Remix | Eartheater, Doss | 3:43 |
| Midnight Morning | Menahan Street Band | 2:57 |
| Ebullient Trap Music | AXS Music | 2:39 |
| Fireworks | Zeeko | 2:37 |
| Low Tide | Tom Rhodes, Hustle Standard | 3:59 |
| 6 Encores for Piano: No. 3, Wasserklavier | Marino Formenti | 2:20 |
| Mên-an-Tol | Mark Pritchard | 1:32 |
| All In Circles | Shida Shahabi | 3:57 |
| **Roi – Instrumental** | **Mckyyy** | **1:23** |
| I Love U/F U | Antonio.609 | 3:23 |
| When Everything Was New | Christian Löffler | 4:27 |
| Memory Arc | Rival Consoles | 2:13 |
| The Sea in Your Eyes | Gigi Masin, Johnny Nash | 2:56 |

**1hr 46m**

# (Addiction) [Cocaine]

| | | |
|---|---|---|
| This Trumpet in My Head | Lykke Li | 1:42 |
| She's Your Cocaine | Tori Amos | 3:42 |
| Pure Cocaine | Lil Baby | 2:34 |
| Cocaine | Robin Thicke | 3:30 |
| Ghetto Rock | Mos Def | 3:53 |
| Hustlin' | Rick Ross | 4:14 |
| Cocaine | Eric Clapton | 3:42 |
| Cocaine Blues | Escort | 4:08 |
| Dust in a Baggie | Billy Strings | 2:54 |
| Clandestina | FILV, Edmofo, Emma Peters | 2:30 |
| Rehab | Amy Winehouse | 3:34 |
| Here for My Habits | Ängie | 3:14 |
| Pusherman | Curtis Mayfield | 5:01 |
| Cocaine Blues – Live at Folsom State Prison, Folsom, CA (1st Show) | Johnny Cash | 2:49 |
| I Cram to Understand U | MC Lyte | 4:42 |
| Can't Feel My Face | The Weeknd | 3:34 |
| Serious Drug | Wildcookie | 2:56 |
| COCAINE DOLPHINS | French Police | 3:45 |
| Duck Down! | The Roots | 3:56 |
| Cocaine Style | ARO | 3:16 |
| Cocaine Kisses | Leezy | 3:04 |
| My Gasoline | Maddix, Fēlēs | 3:57 |
| Rest My Chemistry | Interpol | 5:01 |
| Dust | Ängie, Tail Whip | 3:32 |
| Sunset | LUCKI | 2:05 |
| Cocaine | CRUCIFIX | 4:30 |
| Cocaine | Dreams We've Had | 6:05 |
| Blow | Beyoncé | 5:10 |
| Edit | Regina Spektor | 4:51 |
| Cocaine | Jim Jones, Philthy Rich | 3:54 |
| Cocaine Cat | Tess Parks, Anton Newcombe | 4:09 |

**1hr 55m**

# (Insomnia) [Without You]

| | | |
|---|---|---|
| Evergreen (You Didn't Deserve Me At All) | Omar Apollo | 3:37 |
| SWEET/I THOUGHT YOU WANTED TO DANCE | Tyler, The Creator, Brent Faiyaz, Fana Hues | 9:48 |
| Noches | Prince Innocence | 3:13 |
| Best to You | Blood Orange | 3:46 |
| All A Mystery | Phantogram | 3:09 |
| Florida Blues | Cruel Youth | 4:24 |
| Beige | TOBi, Harrison | 2:51 |
| New York City | The Chainsmokers | 3:51 |
| At Last I Am Free | Robert Wyatt | 4:17 |
| La flemme | Owlle | 3:03 |
| I Don't Want You Anymore | Cherry Glazerr | 3:29 |
| Falling Away from Me | Korn | 4:31 |
| Selene | Night Tapes | 4:55 |
| Headin' For A Heartache | Juice Newton | 2:45 |
| Gaslight Anthem (The Song Not The Band) | Thin Lips | 3:02 |
| Olympus | Blondshell | 3:37 |
| Can't Be Tamed | Miley Cyrus | 2:48 |
| Shark In The Water | V V Brown | 3:04 |
| Tear in My Heart | Twenty One Pilots | 3:08 |
| I Don't Know You | The Marias | 3:29 |
| Just A Stranger | Kali Uchis, Steve Lacy | 2:58 |
| Your Love Is Like Petrol | Client | 3:14 |
| Maybe You're The Problem | Ava Max | 3:10 |
| Guilty Conscience | 070 Shake | 3:33 |
| Killshot | Magdalena Bay | 3:56 |
| The Wall | PatrickReza | 3:16 |
| **WITHOUT YOU** | **The Kid LAROI** | **2:41** |
| Love Is A Losing Game – Original Demo | Amy Winehouse | 3:44 |
| I Was a Fool – Monsieur Adi Remix | Tegan and Sara, Monsieur Adi | 4:31 |
| Supercut | Lorde | 4:38 |
| Marilyn Monroe | Sevdaliza | 3:29 |

1hr 55m

# (Adonis) [Captain Save a Hoe]

| Roads | Portishead | 5:04 |
|---|---|---|
| SEX | Mötley Crüe | 3:41 |
| Eighth Wonder of the World | Cathedral Bells | 2:08 |
| The Wreck of the Edmund Fitzgerald | Gordon Lightfoot | 6:29 |
| Every Breaking Wave | U2 | 4:12 |
| Someone Saved My Life Tonight | Elton John | 6:45 |
| Tomorrow Never Knows | The Beatles | 3:00 |
| Vamos a la Playa – 1983 | Righeira | 3:37 |
| Anything's Possible | Lea Michele | 3:46 |
| Captain | MiyaGi | 3:34 |
| I've Been Everywhere | Johnny Cash | 3:17 |
| Pleasant Street | Tim Buckley | 5:17 |
| Cape St Vincent | Pram | 3:33 |
| Wind Of Change | Scorpions | 5:12 |
| My Blood | Twenty One Pilots | 3:49 |
| My Sweet Prince | Placebo | 5:45 |
| Captain Hook | Megan Thee Stallion | 2:57 |
| Breathe (In the Air) | Pink Floyd | 2:50 |
| A Trip Through Space to Clear My Mind | Tanerélle | 3:42 |
| LOST FOREVER | Travis Scott, Westside Gunn | 2:43 |
| Captain Save Uh Oh | Fresh X Reckless | 2:09 |
| Play With Fire | Nico Santos | 3:34 |
| The Captain | HIJCKD | 3:12 |
| Water Under The Bridge | Thievery Corporation, Natalia Clavier | 4:47 |
| Whirlpool | Seal | 3:58 |
| Sail | AWOLNATION | 4:19 |
| **Captain Save A Hoe** | **E-40, The Click, Suga T, D-Shott, B-Legit** | **4:48** |
| Things We Do For Love | Horace Brown | 4:58 |
| Policy of Truth | Depeche Mode | 4:55 |
| Do That To Me One More Time | Captain & Tennille | 4:17 |
| CaptainOverboard | BONES, GREAF | 1:35 |

**2hr 3m**

# (Fucking) [Bite the Pillow]

| | | |
|---|---|---|
| Lost in the Fire | Gesaffelstein, The Weeknd | 3:22 |
| Rough Sex | Lords Of Acid | 4:50 |
| Look Back At Me | Trina, Killer Mike | 4:13 |
| Pussy (Real Good) | Jacki-O, Rodney | 4:24 |
| Sex Talk | Megan Thee Stallion | 2:11 |
| Rodeo (Remix) | Lah Pat, Flo Milli | 4:06 |
| I Fucking Lust You | D'african | 2:44 |
| Mini Mini | Punto40, Marcianeke | 3:18 |
| Sl*t Him Out Again | Baby Tate, Kaliii | 3:53 |
| Comme un boomerang | Serge Gainsbourg | 2:40 |
| Overnight Sensation | BØRNS | 3:18 |
| Whoregasm | cupcakKe | 3:58 |
| Throat Goat | Kim Petras | 2:20 |
| Talk Dirty | Jason Derulo, 2Chainz | 2:58 |
| Eat It Up | Kaliii, BIA | 3:02 |
| My Type | Saweetie, Jhené Aiko, City Girls | 2:52 |
| Cock | Spice | 2:48 |
| Bring on the Nubiles | The Stranglers | 2:16 |
| Another Nasty Song | Latto | 2:24 |
| Truth Or Dare | Kelela | 4:12 |
| Twerk | City Girls, Cardi B | 2:46 |
| Rough Sex | Tay GMBO | 2:02 |
| Harder Now | Louisahhh, Wax Wings | 4:30 |
| TASTY | Shygirl | 2:24 |
| Bend It Over | Renni Rucci | 2:56 |
| Animal (Fuck Like A Beast) | W.A.S.P. | 3:07 |
| **Bite the Pillow** | **ATG Sheed** | **2:12** |
| I Love It (& Lil Pump) | Kanye West, Lil Pump | 2:08 |
| THIQUE | Beyoncé | 4:05 |
| Lights Down Low | Maejor, Waka Flocka Flame | 3:06 |
| Turn Down the Lights | Kranium | 3:12 |

**1hr 38m**

# (Selene) [Heavy Dirty Soul]

| | | |
|---|---|---|
| The Chain | Fleetwood Mac | 4:30 |
| Hex Girl | Moon Sisters, The Nostalgia Girls | 1:41 |
| Malignant | Ed Tullett | 5:18 |
| Wine & Spirits | 070 Shake | 3:16 |
| Demons | Doja Cat | 3:16 |
| In Her Arms You Will Never Starve | Copeland | 4:57 |
| Pan's Labyrinth Lullaby | Javier Navarrete | 1:48 |
| Supermassive Black Hole | Muse | 3:32 |
| I Bet on Losing Dogs | Mitski | 2:50 |
| In Noctem | Nicholas Hooper | 2:01 |
| Raised By Wolves | U2 | 4:06 |
| Night Train | Nomy | 4:47 |
| Nightcrawler | Nosaj Thing | 3:46 |
| Lose Your Soul | Dead Man's Bones | 4:35 |
| Black Dress | 070 Shake | 3:57 |
| Artemis | AURORA | 2:39 |
| Rosyln | Bon Iver, St. Vincent | 4:50 |
| Dark Matter | Andrew Belle | 5:18 |
| I Got 5 On It (Tethered Mix from US) | Michael Abels, Luniz, Michael Marshall | 1:43 |
| Undisclosed Desires | Muse | 3:55 |
| Glory Box | Portishead | 5:09 |
| Burn the Witch | Radiohead | 3:41 |
| The Labyrinth | Javier Navarrete | 4:07 |
| Madness | Muse | 4:41 |
| Bury It | CHVRCHES | 3:09 |
| You should see me in a crown | Billie Eilish | 3:01 |
| **Heavydirtysoul** | **Twenty One Pilots** | **3:55** |
| Midnight love | girl in red | 3:14 |
| With You In My Head | UNKLE, The Black Angels | 5:12 |
| Paint The Town Red | Doja Cat | 3:50 |
| It's All in Vain | Wet | 3:34 |

**1hr 56m**

# (Defeat) [Going Home]

| | | |
|---|---|---|
| The 49th Day | El Ten Eleven | 4:53 |
| Loving on Moon | r mccarthy | 2:01 |
| Cassius | Elliott Yorke | 4:33 |
| From My Soul | Kieran Jandu | 6:15 |
| Aftermath | Nine Inch Nails | 2:26 |
| The Hourglass | Ben Crosland | 2:00 |
| Photograph | Perfume Genius | 4:41 |
| Phoenix | Daft Punk | 4:57 |
| A Walk | Tycho | 5:16 |
| Quarto de Hotel | Hareton Salvanini | 2:42 |
| Stepping Through Shadow | Menahan Street Band | 2:01 |
| Fall From Heaven | Artonoise | 7:14 |
| Passage Through The Spheres | Kali Malone, Etienne Ferchaud | 6:48 |
| Ain't That Peculiar | Ramsey Lewis | 2:57 |
| Sabbat, pt. 1 | Cortex | 1:01 |
| Captain | Gaspard Augé, Justice | 3:22 |
| Seiko 3 | Yasuaki Shimizu | 1:17 |
| Terror Island – Mushrooms Project Mix | Billy Bogus, Mushrooms Project | 5:50 |
| Where Is My Mind? | Tkay Maidza | 2:57 |
| Double Happiness | Terence Blanchard | 6:08 |
| Dancer In The Dark | Björk Björk, Vienna Horns | 3:55 |
| Flares | NIVIRO | 3:25 |
| Purple Rose Minuet | Susumu Yokota | 3:36 |
| Keyboard Song | ARTHUR | 2:21 |
| The Marble Eye | Anna von Hausswolff | 5:18 |
| Decency | Tide Electric | 2:35 |
| **Going Home** | **Alice Coltrane** | **10:01** |
| Lady Love | Piero Piccioni | 1:57 |
| PS | Ej Hoffman | 2:35 |
| Cherry Blossom | Emancipator, Koresma | 3:01 |
| Seeing Beauty in Everything | Ky akasha | 2:21 |

**2hr**

# (Hate) [Cherry]

| Master of None | Beach House | 3:19 |
| --- | --- | --- |
| Sex & Sativa | Miah Fuego | 3:10 |
| Disclaimer | Libel | 3:14 |
| Bad News | Kanye West | 3:59 |
| Sober II (Melodrama) | Lorde | 2:59 |
| No Going Back | Yuno | 3:28 |
| Voice of the Soul | Death | 3:44 |
| Dead To Me | Chloe Adams | 2:33 |
| Leave You Lonely | Tara Carosielli | 2:53 |
| Petite fille princesse | Les Rita Mitsouko | 3:27 |
| Needed Me | Rihanna | 3:12 |
| I hope that you think of me | Pity Party (Girls Club), Lucys | 2:08 |
| Selene | Michael Manring | 4:53 |
| Fatal Attraction | Kevin Gates | 2:49 |
| Fuck Me Pumps | Amy Winehouse | 3:21 |
| Hatefuck | Cruel Youth | 4:04 |
| SLUT ME OUT 2 | NLE Choppa | 2:15 |
| Without You | ODESZA | 3:04 |
| A Storm That Took Everything | Thom Yorke | 1:48 |
| Girl With The Tattoo Enter.lewd | Miguel | 1:43 |
| Pimper's Paradise | Bob Marley & The Wailers | 3:28 |
| Dark Side Of The Moon | suisside | 2:49 |
| Neon Rouge (Outro) | Jimmy Whoo | 2:52 |
| We Still Don't Trust You | Future, Metro Boomin, The Weeknd | 4:13 |
| Emily – Rough Mix | My Chemical Romance | 3:12 |
| Burn The Witch | PVRIS, Tommy Genesis, Alice Longyu Gao | 2:56 |
| **Cherry** | **Chromatics** | **4:32** |
| Bad Juju | YULLOLA | 2:06 |
| I Don't Want You On My Mind | Bill Withers | 4:37 |
| What's a Girl to Do? | Bat For Lashes | 2:59 |
| Gem Lingo (ovr now) | Overmono, Ruthven | 3:50 |

1hr 39m

# (Voodoo Pussy) [Rump Punch]

| | | |
|---|---|---|
| Pussy Talk | City Girls, Doja Cat | 3:38 |
| Awesome Jawsome | Sexyy Red | 2:49 |
| XXXTC | Brooke Candy, Charli xcx, Maliibu Mitch | 3:18 |
| Voodoo Pussy | LSDXOXO | 3:23 |
| Big Racks | Bree Runway, Brooke Candy | 3:04 |
| Show Me Something | Renni Rucci | 2:11 |
| Heaven's Little Bastard | BbyMutha | 2:25 |
| Play With It | Tommy Genesis | 2:00 |
| Pink Birthday | Nicki Minaj | 2:08 |
| Play | Alewya | 3:21 |
| Lick Me | Sexyy Red, Lil Baby | 2:28 |
| Mhmm (Enchanted) | $wizzz | 3:06 |
| Doom | Blac Chyna, Asian Doll | 2:49 |
| Cookie | R. Kelly | 3:45 |
| Make That Cake | LunchMoney Lewis, Doja Cat | 2:53 |
| Sugar Mama | Dua Saleh | 2:17 |
| LUNCH | Billie Eilish | 2:59 |
| Chun Swae | Nicki Minaj, Swae Lee | 6:10 |
| MMM MMM | Kaliii, ATL Jacob | 2:17 |
| FENTY SEX | Smino, Dreezy | 3:34 |
| Drip | Brooke Candy, Erika Jayne | 2:13 |
| Rodeo | City Girls | 2:57 |
| Blush | Siena Liggins | 2:41 |
| Girl Crush | Boys Noize, Rico Nasty | 3:48 |
| Clitopia | Dorian Electra | 3:49 |
| Bitches | Tove Lo | 2:17 |
| **Rump Punch** | **Cash Cobain** | **2:03** |
| Funnel Of Love | SQÜRL, Madeline Follin | 3:40 |
| Candy | Foxy Brown, Kelis | 3:43 |
| Guess | Charli xcx, Billie Eilish | 2:23 |
| Rakata | Arca | 2:31 |

1hr 32m

# (Road Trip) [Nightdrive with You]

| | | |
|---|---|---|
| Headlock | Imogen Heap | 3:35 |
| Sex | Kix | 3:56 |
| You're Mine | Phantogram | 2:51 |
| Sweater Weather | The Neighbourhood | 4:00 |
| Moanin' and Groanin' | Bill Withers | 2:58 |
| A Better Way To Love | Gone Gone Beyond | 4:23 |
| Death Note | Hideki Taniuchi | 3:10 |
| Contortion | Sextile | 3:11 |
| Ride a White Horse – Single Version | Goldfrapp | 3:44 |
| Brujo Magic – Apophenia Edit | Suns of Arqa | 4:56 |
| Midnight Moon | Oh Wonder | 3:30 |
| Fall Into Place | TAAHLIAH, Tsatsamis | 3:32 |
| Dusk to Dawn | Emancipator | 5:25 |
| Midnight Rendezvous | The Babys | 3:36 |
| Without You | Kygo, HAYLA | 4:23 |
| Burning Desire | Lana Del Rey | 3:51 |
| Ride | Ciara, Ludacris | 4:34 |
| Weird Fishes / Arpeggi | Radiohead | 5:18 |
| Akira The Wild | Kensuke Ushio | 1:55 |
| Intro | Orion Sun | 3:00 |
| Lapdance from Asia | Cosha, Shygirl | 3:28 |
| Light It Up | Topic, Jona Selle | 3:59 |
| That 'just got home from work' type of beat | charlie toØ human | 2:03 |
| The Taste of You | Ritual Howls | 4:12 |
| Texas Sun | Khruangbin, Leon Bridges | 4:12 |
| Because the Night | Patti Smith | 3:25 |
| **Nightdrive with You (Fear Of Tigers Remix)** | **Anoraak, Fear Of Tigers** | **5:55** |
| Love In Space | Cherry Bullet | 3:36 |
| Garden Kisses | GIVĒON | 3:15 |
| Do You Feel High? | Pink Skies | 3:15 |
| Lost | Maroon 5 | 2:52 |

**1hr 56m**

# (Beyond Green) [Into The Freedom]

| | | |
|---|---|---|
| Atom 13 | Sleeping At Last | 1:00 |
| Yirga | Flughand | 1:47 |
| Olson | Boards of Canada | 1:32 |
| Emancipation | Helios | 2:35 |
| Dewdrops | Gaussian Curve | 1:45 |
| Piano Piece | Clan of Xymox | 1:29 |
| Mountains Crave | Anna von Hausswolff | 3:35 |
| SUNRISE (Slowed + Reverb) | Xantesha | 2:19 |
| January | Loving | 1:54 |
| Five Hundred Miles | Mamman Sani | 5:53 |
| Phantom | Vestron Vulture | 3:18 |
| A Ritual for Saying Goodbye | Jim Perkins, Joanna Forbes L'Estrange | 1:47 |
| ムーンライト伝説 (Japanese Version) | Salomé Anjari | 3:06 |
| Parallel Universe | Tevvez | 3:25 |
| Kala | Ali Farka Touré, Toumani Diabaté | 5:05 |
| Fleeting Smile | Roger Eno | 2:30 |
| Liquid Spear Waltz | Michael Andrews | 1:34 |
| Minus One | Broadcast | 2:02 |
| The stars vs creatures | Colleen | 5:14 |
| Where Is My Mind? – Piano | Kindt | 3:28 |
| Eros | Nicholas Britell | 3:15 |
| We All Turn to Stars | God Body Disconnect | 4:24 |
| Bollywood Apologetics | Black Wing | 5:36 |
| Heart Cry | Drehz | 2:40 |
| Collette | The Durutti Column | 2:23 |
| Diabolos | STRAIGHT RAZOR | 3:43 |
| **Into The Freedom** | **Uyama Hiroto** | **1:25** |
| Beyond Love | Lance Takamiya | 2:45 |
| Epilogue | Jóhann Jóhannsson | 1:49 |
| Harpsichord Kiss | Martina Topley-Bird | 0:59 |
| See You Tomorrow | Evgeny Grinko | 1:31 |

**1hr 25m**

# (Selene) [Forget]

| | | |
|---|---|---|
| Welcome to the Black Parade | My Chemical Romance | 5:11 |
| Sexy Villain | Remi Wolf | 3:09 |
| Gaslight | fDeluxe | 4:19 |
| The Girl Who Lost the World | YULLOLA | 2:04 |
| Bullets | NEEDTOBREATHE | 3:15 |
| The Art of Survival | Ramsey | 4:20 |
| Yamaha | Delta Spirit | 4:24 |
| (I Just) Died In Your Arms | Cutting Crew | 4:39 |
| TMW | Avenoir | 2:09 |
| Talagh | Googoosh | 4:47 |
| I Don't Love You | Cruel Youth | 3:19 |
| Fall In Love | Phantogram | 3:43 |
| Medusa | Kailee Morgue | 3:23 |
| Tainted Love | Soft Cell | 2:34 |
| Gemini Feed | BANKS | 3:06 |
| Liar | sundial | 2:14 |
| Pussy | Lady | 3:13 |
| Bitch Bites Dog | Cecile Believe | 3:32 |
| Cinema | Sabina Sciubba | 3:51 |
| She Wants To (Get on Down) | Bill Withers | 3:15 |
| Crystal Poles | Scarlett Taylor | 4:43 |
| Love The Way You Lie | Eminem, Rihanna | 4:23 |
| Freedom | Elle Valenci | 3:00 |
| Without you | Isabel LaRosa | 2:37 |
| Lovefool | No Vacation | 2:11 |
| My Kink Is Karma | Chappell Roan | 3:43 |
| **Forget** | **Fashion Club, Perfume Genius** | **3:27** |
| But babe, you love being gaslit | homewrckers | 2:33 |
| Hard Feelings/Loveless | Lorde | 6:07 |
| Moon River | Frank Ocean | 3:08 |
| Lost In The Light | Bahamas | 3:57 |

1hr 50m

# (Soul Nebula) [Wait]

| | | |
|---|---|---|
| Alt Eg Såg | Sigvart Dagsland | 4:24 |
| Fumo Denso | DJ Ride, Capicua | 3:31 |
| 愛已死 (Love Is Dead) | J.Sheon | 4:10 |
| Ἄγγιγμα Ψυχής | Μιχάλης Χατζηγιάννης | 3:12 |
| Non c'è più musica | Mr.Rain, Birdy | 3:31 |
| Ebullient Future – Japanese | ELISA | 3:41 |
| Vaya con dios | Kali Uchis | 2:56 |
| Dernière danse | Indila | 3:33 |
| Adio Kerida | Yasmin Levy | 3:43 |
| Amor | Montell Fish | 3:08 |
| Catalina | ROSALÍA | 3:34 |
| ALTROVE | Ultimo | 3:25 |
| Το Αστέρι Μου | Νατάσσα Μποφίλιου | 3:43 |
| Her Şeyi Yak | Duman | 4:30 |
| A Chi | Fausto Leali | 3:05 |
| Sei Lá | Bárbara Tinoco | 3:22 |
| 困兽 (Caged Beast) | Adam Fan | 2:49 |
| Tiburones (Sharks) | PARIS The Prince | 3:20 |
| Tune Jo Na Kaha | Pritam, Mohit Chauhan, Sandeep Shrivastava | 5:10 |
| Mon mec à moi | Patricia Kaas | 4:14 |
| BODY | MINO | 3:19 |
| Bullet | Shi Shi | 2:57 |
| Mentira | João Pedro Pais | 3:29 |
| Bu Şarki Aşka Yazildi | Cem Adrian | 4:10 |
| Galbi | Soapkills | 4:21 |
| VAMPIROS | ROSALÍA, Rauw Alejandro | 2:57 |
| **Bekle Dedi Gitti – Çizik** | **Kaan Tangöze** | **4:37** |
| LOVE SCENARIO | iKON | 3:30 |
| Les filles désir | Vendredi sur Mer | 3:17 |
| Robarte un Beso | Carlos Vives, Sebastian Yatra | 3:15 |
| 本能 (Instinct) | Sheena Ringo | 4:16 |

**1hr 53m**

# (Devil) [Take Me]

| Me and the Devil | Gil Scott-Heron | 3:34 |
|---|---|---|
| Sex to the Devil | Icky Blossoms | 4:54 |
| Ace of Spades | Motörhead | 2:46 |
| Devil in Paradise | Cruel Youth | 4:03 |
| Devil's Paradise | Birth Of Joy | 3:08 |
| Lucifer | Blutengel | 4:52 |
| Lucifer's Waltz | Secession Studios | 3:04 |
| The Devil's Dancers | Oppenheimer Analysis | 3:05 |
| No Fear | Don Louis | 3:28 |
| Lucifer | SHINee | 3:54 |
| Call Me Devil | Friends in Tokyo | 4:10 |
| Falling from Heaven | Ark Patrol | 4:09 |
| Diablo Rojo | Rodrigo y Gabriela | 4:57 |
| Runnin' with the Devil | Van Halen | 3:35 |
| The Devil You Know | X Ambassadors | 4:03 |
| God Lived As a Devil Dog | Foie Gras | 3:57 |
| Devil Like You | Gareth Dunlop | 3:30 |
| Low Lays the Devil | The Veils | 3:18 |
| Lucifer | Rezz | 5:07 |
| Lucifer | Elle Lexxa | 2:59 |
| Devil Is A Woman | Cloudy June | 3:12 |
| Let's Have a Satanic Orgy | Twin Temple | 4:04 |
| Devil's Respite | Menahan Street Band | 3:51 |
| Used to the Darkness | Des Rocs | 4:16 |
| Devil In My Heart | Jimmy Whoo | 3:03 |
| Devil's Den | DEELYLE | 3:51 |
| **Take Me To Hell** | **Chloe Adams** | **2:13** |
| I love you...my Devil | Nikki Idol | 2:01 |
| Sympathy For The Devil | The Rolling Stones | 6:18 |
| Devil Eyes | Hippie Sabotage | 2:11 |
| Kill Of The Night | Gin Wigmore | 3:25 |

**1hr 54m**

# (Acid Trip) [Lay Back]

| | | |
|---|---|---|
| Midnight City | M83 | 4:04 |
| Otra Vez | ProdMarvin | 2:14 |
| Fade to Grey | Visage | 3:59 |
| 1983…(A Merman I Should Turn to Be) | Jimi Hendrix | 13:40 |
| Moon, Turn the Tides…Gently Gently… | Jimi Hendrix | 1:02 |
| Breakthespell | Mk.gee | 4:27 |
| Cold Was the Ground | The Limiñanas | 3:49 |
| KINTSUGI | Steff da Campo, Ilkay Sencan | 2:57 |
| There's A New Day Coming | Menahan Street Band, Saundra Williams | 2:23 |
| Φύγε – Reworks | Χάρις Αλεξίου, LEX | 3:52 |
| GodLovesUgly – Remix | Atmosphere, Zeds Dead, Subtronics | 3:04 |
| Take Me Down | Pearly Drops | 4:04 |
| O Superman | Laurie Anderson | 8:25 |
| Come sta, La Luna | CAN | 5:43 |
| Honeymoon | Rob Curly | 2:06 |
| Check Your Face | Okay Kaya | 2:57 |
| Medusa's Interlude | Alia Kadir | 1:21 |
| Come into the Water | Mitski | 1:32 |
| Mirage | Orion Sun | 0:57 |
| Drip bounce_7_24_18 | Toro y Moi | 2:35 |
| Low – Edit | Lenny Kravitz | 4:00 |
| Viva l'amour | Sabina Sciubba | 3:05 |
| Test & Recognise – Flume Re-work | Seekae | 5:04 |
| Disengage | Acopia | 2:47 |
| Rosebud | U.S. Girls | 3:10 |
| Midnight | Siobhan Sainte | 3:08 |
| **Lay Back** | **CLAVVS** | **3:49** |
| A New Kind Of Love – Demo | Frou Frou, Imogen Heap, Guy Sigsworth | 4:19 |
| Faces | No Swoon | 4:55 |
| I Dream in Neon | Dirty Beaches | 3:36 |
| Outré Lux | Photay, Madison McFerrin | 4:01 |

1hr 57m

# (Kink) [Poly]

| | | |
|---|---|---|
| More/Diamond Ring | benny blanco, Ty Dolla $ign, 6LACK | 3:03 |
| Flowers & Sex | EMELINE, smle | 2:29 |
| She's My Collar | Gorillaz, Kali Uchis | 3:30 |
| Luv Em All | Sleepy Hallow | 2:28 |
| 10 Bad Bitches | Too $hort, Stressmatic | 3:50 |
| Break up with your girlfriend, I'm bored | Ariana Grande | 3:10 |
| Sad Girl | Lana Del Rey | 5:18 |
| Porn Star Dancing | My Darkest Days, Chad Kroeger, Zakk Wylde | 3:19 |
| Girlfriend | Siena Liggins | 2:50 |
| Toda (Remix) | Alex Rose, Rauw Alejandro, et al | 6:08 |
| FREAK IN YOU | PARTYNEXTDOOR | 4:32 |
| House Of Cards | Radiohead | 5:28 |
| Mr. Watson | Cruel Youth | 3:35 |
| Hurricane | Halsey | 3:43 |
| Marriage Is For Old Folks | Nina Simone | 3:29 |
| Don't Tell Daddy | Hotel Sex | 3:36 |
| Dick | StarBoi3, Doja Cat | 2:55 |
| Blood In The Cut | K.Flay | 3:09 |
| DIRTY LITTLE SECRET | Nessa Barrett | 3:35 |
| Lock&Key | Lolahol | 2:58 |
| Freek-A-Leek | Petey Pablo | 3:55 |
| Bottoms Up | Trey Songz, Nicki Minaj | 4:02 |
| Alright | Victoria Monét | 2:54 |
| Lose My Mind | PARTYNEXTDOOR | 3:04 |
| Snatched | Big Boss Vette | 2:40 |
| ADDICTIONS | Brent Faiyaz, Tre' Amani | 3:12 |
| Poly Amor | Tora | 3:23 |
| MY LOVE | HAWA | 3:38 |
| Thot Thoughts | Muni Long, Sukihana | 3:35 |
| BAMBAM | Ängie, Harrison First | 3:06 |
| BABYDOLL | LUNA AURA | 2:46 |

**1hr 49m**

# (Heart in a Box) [Anything You Want]

| | | |
|---|---|---|
| Why Why Why Why Why | SAULT | 3:59 |
| Self Control | Frank Ocean | 4:10 |
| Black Magic Woman | VCTRYS | 3:07 |
| Back to Black | Amy Winehouse | 4:00 |
| Black Mascara. | RAYE | 4:00 |
| See Her Out (That's Just Life) | Francis and the Lights | 3:31 |
| I Wish you Roses | Kali Uchis | 3:40 |
| Honey | 070 Shake, Ralphy River, Hack & Tree | 6:38 |
| Without You | Perfume Genius | 2:36 |
| QQ (QUÉDATE QUERIENDOME) | Tei Shi | 3:21 |
| New Chains, Same Shackles | $uicideboy$ | 2:19 |
| Affection | BETWEEN FRIENDS | 3:55 |
| (You're The) Devil in Disguise | Elvis Presley | 2:20 |
| Time After Time | Cyndi Lauper | 4:01 |
| Are You Gone Already | Nicki Minaj | 4:31 |
| Better Version | Sabrina Claudio | 3:35 |
| Terrible Thing | AG | 3:38 |
| You'll miss me when I'm not around | Grimes | 2:42 |
| Movies | Conan Gray | 3:34 |
| HARDLY EVER SMILE (without you) | POiSON GiRL FRiEND | 6:55 |
| Not My Fault | Reneé Rapp, Megan Thee Stallion | 2:51 |
| Gaslit Fire | Liv Garland | 2:47 |
| The Difference Is Why | Lenny Kravitz | 4:53 |
| Same | Cage The Elephant | 2:58 |
| X | Welshly Arms | 3:47 |
| Circle For A Landing | Three Dog Night | 2:22 |
| **Anything You Want** | **Acopia** | **3:01** |
| Almost Made You Love Me | Boaksi | 7:38 |
| Write This Down | SoulChef, Nieve | 3:09 |
| Sweet Dreams | BØRNS | 3:20 |
| Strange | Celeste | 4:16 |

1hr 57m

# (FFFado) [Lisbon]

| | | |
|---|---|---|
| WBWU | Purient | 3:19 |
| Rinsed | Evoni | 2:58 |
| GASLIGHT GIRLBOSS GATEKEEP | CyberGirlfriend, Baby Brat | 1:59 |
| Nothing Left to Save | CASHFORGOLD, Tim Schaufert | 3:43 |
| Yours & Mine | Lucy Dacus | 5:14 |
| Low Tide | DRAMA | 3:46 |
| No Time To Die | Billie Ellish | 4:02 |
| Behind the Scenes | Zero, Jess Spink | 4:43 |
| Move On | Temm | 3:42 |
| Fado da saudade | Amália Rodrigues | 3:09 |
| Trouble Always Finds Me | Yellow House | 4:02 |
| Fallingwater | Maggie Rogers | 4:31 |
| Doc Whiler | Alex Banin | 2:30 |
| Silver Springs – Live at Warner Brothers Studios in Burbank, CA 5/23/97 | Fleetwood Mac | 5:42 |
| Dance Me to the End of Love | Leonard Cohen | 4:41 |
| Head | claire rousay | 4:44 |
| Sticky | Ravyn Lenae | 3:17 |
| Blood On Your Hands | 070 Shake | 3:35 |
| 999 | Prince Innocence, Harrison | 2:48 |
| Who Do You Want | Ex Habit | 2:20 |
| Selene | NIKI | 3:17 |
| Resurrection | MOTHERMARY | 2:50 |
| Romantic Homicide | d4vd | 2:13 |
| Numb | Men I Trust | 3:39 |
| Soft Spot | Claud | 3:08 |
| Running with the Wolves | AURORA | 3:15 |
| **Lisbon** | **Wolf Alice** | **3:26** |
| Love | Keyshia Cole | 4:15 |
| Diary | Bread | 3:09 |
| Move On | Mandy Patinkin, Bernadette Peters | 3:39 |
| Love Alone | Anachnid | 4:06 |

**1hr 51m**

# (Kintsugi) [Aftercare]

| | | |
|---|---|---|
| New Dawn | Gaby Moreno | 3:25 |
| Water Over Sex | Lala Lala | 2:50 |
| Kintsugi | Good Lee, Jade Alice | 4:10 |
| liMOusIne | Bring Me The Horizon, AURORA | 4:12 |
| Go(l)d | Mereba | 3:23 |
| How I Get Myself Killed | Indigo De Souza | 3:16 |
| Unmoored | Fog Chaser | 2:31 |
| Move | Saint Motel | 3:08 |
| Coast | Hailee Steinfeld, Anderson.Paak | 2:47 |
| La luna enamorada | Kali Uchis | 1:51 |
| Adorn | You'll Never Get to Heaven | 4:25 |
| Going Under | Evanescence | 3:35 |
| Kintsugi | DROELOE | 3:29 |
| Gold Dust Woman | Fleetwood Mac | 4:56 |
| Little by Little | The Marias | 2:58 |
| You're My Latest, My Greatest Inspiration | Teddy Pendergrass | 5:21 |
| Pluto | Björk | 3:19 |
| You'll Find A Way (Switch and Sinden Remix) | Santigold | 3:13 |
| The Struggle for Ebullience | Carter Burwell | 1:35 |
| Kintsugi | Gabrielle Aplin | 2:56 |
| Baby Don't Hurt Me | David Guetta, Anne-Marie, Coi Leray | 2:20 |
| The Melting Of The Sun | St. Vincent | 4:18 |
| Ebullience | Tini Mc | 4:06 |
| The Lights of Town | Cemeteries | 2:59 |
| Different This Time | Cornelia Murr | 3:53 |
| Fever | Sherwyn, Sariah Mae | 2:58 |
| **Aftercare** | **Twelve25** | **3:20** |
| Give Me Your Love | The Babys | 3:37 |
| Serenity | Godsmack | 4:35 |
| An Explanation for That Flock of Crows | Algebra Suicide | 2:44 |
| Pieces Of You | 070 Shake | 2:48 |

**1hr 44m**

# Reading Between Lines

*I Can See Clearly Now | Johnny Nash*

Money = Power
Active Listening = Control
Doing what you want = Freedom
Persuading others = Agency

Being heard = Subjectify
Being seen = Objectify
Star = Protagonist
Life = Movie

To get someone talking = Interrogate
Actor = Baby (or Sugar Baby)
Giving a monologue = Giving head
Producer = Daddy (or Sugar Daddy)

Narrative = Arc of relationship
Actor/Producer = Sub/Dom

(P.S. The bewitched man has come to be treated by black magic as DADDY)

*(Beyond Love)*

Champagne Room | Sizzy Rocket

# After life

**MONSIEUR:** Il y a dans l'être
quelque chose de particulièrement tentant pour l'homme
et ce quelque chose est justement
LE CACA.
(Ici rugissements.)

> [Playa Alicia]
>
> **SWIM
> AT OWN
> RISK**

**MÔMO:**   dans la crasse
             d'un paradis

# (Silhouettes

# *of* cheet *a a a* h s)

> [Cheetah cage]
>
> **ENTER
> AT OWN
> RISK**

**MÔMO:**   Mais est-ce que je n'y suis pas entré
             dans cette foutue branleuse vie
             depuis cinquante ans que je suis né.

# PACMAN NEBULA

**It's Complicated** | **Sassy 009**

**ADONIS:** I upended my life to be with you.

**SELENE:** I know.

**ADONIS:** Then I upended it to escape you.

**SELENE:** That hurts.

**ADONIS:** Me too.

**SELENE:** Come back.

**ADONIS:** I can't.

**SELENE:** You can.

**ADONIS:** You don't want me.

**SELENE:** I do.

**ADONIS:** You resent me.

**SELENE:** I don't trust you.

**ADONIS:** You don't love me.

**SELENE:** I do. But I don't know how.

**ADONIS:** No, that's not it.

**SELENE:** It is.

**ADONIS:** No. You don't know how to be loved.

**SELENE:** (Crying)

**ADONIS:** The way you love is irresistible. The way you receive love is vengeful.

**SELENE:** I hate myself.

**ADONIS:** You shouldn't.

**SELENE:** But I do.

**ADONIS:** That's why you hate being loved.

**SELENE:** Why?

**ADONIS:** You're not used to it.

**SELENE:** (Imploring) Come back.

**ADONIS:** (Fleeing)

(P.S. It means the ending of an era and in Selene's case the lowering of her performance)

# My Afflictions/My Menace (My Altar)

YULLOLA | You Don't Need to Sin to Win My Love

*THE NEED TO BE NEEDED (constantly renewed)*

*CHASING A HIGH/THE SUBLIME (through intimacy)*

*Intimacy = Sex + Affection (post-coital cuddling)*

*CHASING VALIDATION (through romance)*

*SEX AS THERAPY (to heal or to distract?)*

Taping them to my wall
above my writing desk

which is also my altar
where I burn incense

have framed photos
of *The New Night* (2016)

me floating in an infinity pool
overlooking Montego Bay (2024)

a short stack of books (Acker, Artaud, Kraus, Kundera)
forever circulating

a ceramic skull with gaping mouth
I place a sponge inside

as tongue-in-cheek
and on the tongue a white pill

crowned by computer and keyboard
cluttered by myriad papers

*"Beware the undercover producer as lover"*

*GOEW = the melodrama of a breakdown*

*CG = the double tragedy of a con gone awry & a love shattered*

*SWIMMING IN OCEAN = REBIRTH (baptism)*

*THE NEED TO BE NEEDED (I see it now)*

'God! Fuck! Sigh!'
uttered, it becomes art

swallowed, it becomes internalized
internalized, it becomes a super moon

a super moon is exactly what you want
a cycle of new stars and self-loathing

the cycle convinces you you're unlovable
the conviction justifies your (preemptive) deceit

the stars retreat (or die from rejection)
you take pride in this

you assign your identity
a magic from this

a black magic
outside your full control

I don't regret leaving you
by that time, you had already left me

except you didn't tell me

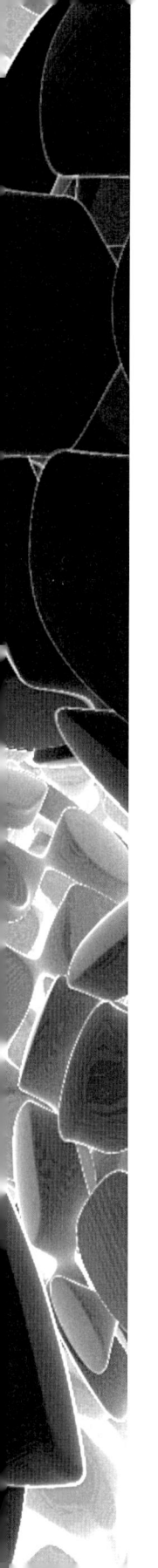

*IRRESISTABLE = IRRECOVERABLE (eventually)*

That's ok though, I like being the last to know
I like having a witch in my bed

      it requires only despair

*More than*   THE NEED TO BE NEEDED   *is*   THE NEED TO FEEL SPECIAL

*More than*   THE NEED TO BE LOVED   *is*   THE NEED TO BE LOVED
                                                                           BY
                                                                  THE MOST
                                                                 UNLIKELY
                                                                   SOURCE

(P.S. A great cry)

# (Scenes & Poems) Of GOEW

*What Fiction Is For | DYAN*

The scenes require you to submit
To the surreal
Not to get caught in illogic

The poems are monologues
But not always clear
Who's speaking

In some cases
It's plausible
It could be one of three characters

In other cases
It's less a mystery of who's speaking
& more a question of setting

The overall structure
Nonlinear & sparse in context
Is meant to immerse you

It doesn't spoil anything
To tell you it's a love story—
Fragments of & its collateral damage

(P.S. It means an air of tragedy)

# WIZARD NEBULA

**The Cut That Always Bleeds | Conan Gray**

**SELENE:** I upended my life for you.

**ADONIS:** I know.

**SELENE:** I regret putting you first.

**ADONIS:** That hurts.

**SELENE:** Me too. I lost lovers.

**ADONIS:** That's not my fault.

**SELENE:** It is.

**ADONIS:** No way.

**SELENE:** You detained me with gifts.

**ADONIS:** I adored you.

**SELENE:** You drowned me. I couldn't swim away.

**ADONIS:** I didn't.

**SELENE:** You did.

**ADONIS:** I tried to help you. But I didn't know how.

**SELENE:** No, that's not it.

**ADONIS:** It is.

**SELENE:** No. You assumed I needed help.

**ADONIS:** (Crying)

**SELENE:** The way you help is punishing. The way you assume is self-serving.

**ADONIS:** I can't help myself.

**SELENE:** You can.

**ADONIS:** I need help. Real love.

**SELENE:** You need sex. To de-stress.

**ADONIS:** Why is that so bad? If you love me?

**SELENE:** That's not love.

**ADONIS:** (Imploring) Come back.

**SELENE:** (Flying)

(P.S. If this held-in gasp is the last then it's time for taking stock then it's true one is going to die or is dead already)

# Afterlife

When Chanty spoke the word
she meant it as metaphor
for sex work

I slowly realized
this woman is a vampire
with a conscience

like me
she didn't want the afterlife
anymore

she said
she had two boys
she wanted life

she made a heart
with her hands
I quickly realized

she meant it as metaphor
for marriage
here I am again

between two worlds
life & afterlife
faced with a choice

the same choice
not yes or no
but for how long?

Every time I step into
the afterlife
to suck the blood

of a demon nymph
I don't kill them
I don't immortalize them

rather
I bring them back
as my wife

this is my cage
I cannot kill
I cannot be saved

(P.S. Go ahead and die, my darling)

# CHAMPAGNE ROOM

**Trap, SAINt JHN | Lil Baby**

**ADONIS:** I like to role play.

**CHANTY:** Puedo ser humana.

**ADONIS:** I like to play God.

**CHANTY:** Puedo ser diabla.

**ADONIS:** No.

**CHANTY:** ¿Qué entonces?

**ADONIS:** Good Cop, Bad Cop.

**CHANTY:** Puedo ser tu prisionera.

**ADONIS:** I have to interrogate you.

**CHANTY:** ¿Qué hice?

**ADONIS:** We're going to find out.

**CHANTY:** No será fácil.

**ADONIS:** I'll torture you.

**CHANTY:** Me gusta el dolor.

**ADONIS:** Afterwards, I'll console you.

**CHANTY:** Papi.

**ADONIS:** Baby.

**CHANTY:** (Purring)

**ADONIS:** I have a question.

**CHANTY:** Sí, mi amor.

**ADONIS:** (Turning her) Have you ever loved someone who didn't love you back?

**CHANTY:** (Spreading her ass) Sí, muchas veces.

**ADONIS:** (Entering her) I see you.

**CHANTY:** (Moaning)

**ADONIS:** You feel good.

**CHANTY:** (Groaning)

**ADONIS:** You sound good.

**CHANTY:** (Panting) Leche.

**ADONIS:** No one dies.

**CHANTY:** (Moaning) Leche.

**ADONIS:** (Plowing) No one comes back.

**CHANTY:** (Groaning) Leche.

**ADONIS:** (Covering her mouth) Shhh.

**CHANTY:** (Panting)

**ADONIS:** I'm coming...

**SECURITY GUARD:** (Knocking) Vamos! Es hora!

**ADONIS:** (Roaring)

(P.S. It means he is tethered between duty and desire)

# Three Guys Walk Into A Bar

*Bathroom | Montell Fish*

Adonis, Rich Man, Bartender
Adonis orders a beer

Rich Man orders a rye
Bartender orders a seltzer, no lime

Chanty approaches Bartender
*What are you drinking?* she asks

He says, *Seltzer water*
She says, *Too weak*

She goes to Rich Man
*What are you drinking?* she asks

He says, *Whiskey*
She says, *Too strong*

She goes to Adonis
*What are you drinking?* she asks

He says, *American imperial porter*
She says, *Just perfect, my life*

And when she says *my life*
She puts her hand on his cock


(P.S. Si mi amor entonces mi vida entonces mi culpa)

# Guide to Trap a Gringo

**Bilingual | Jarina De Marco**

¿Qué estás bebiendo?
*What are you drinking?*

Demasiado débil.
*Too weak.*

Demasiado fuerte.
*Too strong.*

Simplemente perfecto, mi vida.
*Just perfect, my life.*

(P.S. Bathroom stall graffiti)

# BARTENDER
**Skylark** | **Art Blakey**

**RICH MAN:** Where've you been?

**ADONIS:** With the cheetahs, in the cheetah cage.

**RICH MAN:** Ha, you never learn.

**ADONIS:** Oh, I learn. I just don't stop learning. When everyone else stops, I keep going.

**RICH MAN:** Everyone else stops because they see a cliff ahead.

**ADONIS:** Beyond the cliff is where the real learning happens.

**RICH MAN:** It's where men die! No one comes back from the dead, you realize that?

**ADONIS:** How do you define death?

**RICH MAN:** Being broke. You know, poor.

**ADONIS:** Hm!

**RICH MAN:** Speaking of which, there's the matter of your debt.

**ADONIS:** I can buy you a drink, and tell you a story. That's all I got.

**RICH MAN:** I'm not in the business of stories. But you can buy me a drink, and tell me what you know about Selene.

**ADONIS:** (Alarmed) Not your type.

**RICH MAN:** How's that?

**ADONIS:** She's beyond broke. You know, dead.

**RICH MAN:** I'm in the business of saving lives, haven't you heard?

**ADONIS:** No.

**RICH MAN:** I thought she was the love of your life.

**ADONIS:** (Defeated) I thought so too. But what she was...

**RICH MAN:** Well, spit it out.

**ADONIS:** Was a mirror.

**RICH MAN:** Huh?

**ADONIS:** A mirror is the best teacher.

**RICH MAN:** A mirror is for shaving.

**ADONIS:** Do you know what I see when I look in the mirror?

**RICH MAN:** No. Enlighten me.

**ADONIS:** I see a wounded animal. That can't be tamed. But everyone else sees a house pet.

**RICH MAN:** I see a subpoena. (Serves him) And a fool! (Gulps) Thanks for the drink. (Exits)

**BARTENDER:** (Intervening) I see a wounded animal.

**ADONIS:** (Seeing) That wants to heal.

**BARTENDER:** (Seeing) That wants revenge.


(P.S. If she calls she's initiating her revenge then respond with love otherwise don't call then beware the cheetah in lobby)

# No Swimming

*Phoenix | Anachnid*

I am not Antonin Artaud and
I did not go through electroshock but
This is what I saw on the shore of Playa Alicia

A man broke his neck in the surf
Muted sirens and stunned onlookers
Daughters in bikinis adrift, ruined, wrecked

I died with this man in Sosúa
I died five times under black magic
I died figuratively and rightfully

Shock lasts fifteen minutes
Paralysis a half hour or more and then
A lifetime

Now one hour after the incident
I swim in the ocean
Such is my need to break the spell

I have a good memory
Especially of my deaths
But I base my testimony in poetry

I am not a credible witness
I focus on the emotions
Not the details

A policeman on the shore instructs me
To come out of the water
I have yet to break the spell though

I have a sharp recollection of the daughters
How they quivered

In the mind of a dying man
There are more than 10,000 poems
From which I pick one out

I do this five times
To comprise the infected nucleus

There is consensus among family, friends, lovers
The dead man must not come back to life
Until the insurance is paid out

And what do you expect a dead man to do
Except to be reborn?

I would prefer to raise a dead lover
Than to resurrect myself
This is the difference between a god and a vampire

A god is a saint
A vampire is a narcissist

Black magic is powerful
I am adrift, ruined, wrecked
I do not know if I'm going to make it to shore

All 10,000 poems turn inward
Against me

(P.S. It means in pursuit of something religious there's
a strong riptide)

# OSCAR ACCEPTANCE SPEECH
**Never Say Never Again | Lani Hall**

(In attendance with Selene)

**ANNOUNCER:** And the Oscar for 'Best Original Screenplay' goes to... Adonis, for the Adonis Saga. (Applause)

(Projection:)

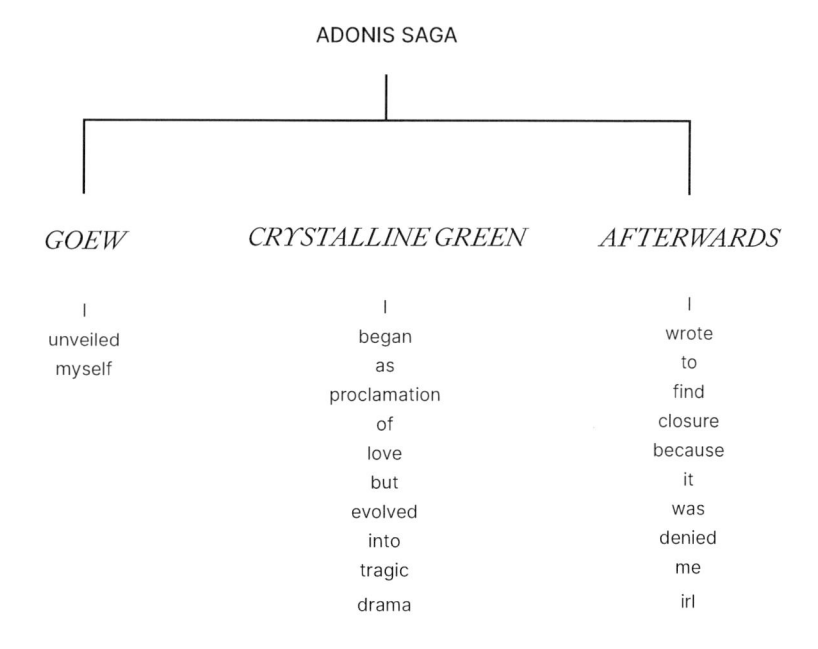

ADONIS SAGA

| *GOEW* | *CRYSTALLINE GREEN* | *AFTERWARDS* |
|---|---|---|
| I | I | I |
| unveiled | began | wrote |
| myself | as | to |
|  | proclamation | find |
|  | of | closure |
|  | love | because |
|  | but | it |
|  | evolved | was |
|  | into | denied |
|  | tragic | me |
|  | drama | irl |

I accept blue or turquoise as the "green" of each window. If you have spent time in the city, any city, you know there are countless windows, that they are more grey than green, or blue. But at certain time of day, with certain interior lighting, at certain angle, they appear green, fertile, and inviting. A forest of diffuse light. I like to contrast this against the impression of a concrete jungle.

(Adonis ascends stage)

**ADONIS:** Writers are only as good as their muses. Films are only as good as their actors. Life is only as good as your current lover. Or lovers. It's ok to have multiple lovers. Though, be careful who you let into your bedroom, and who you keep in your inner circle. And be honest. Be fully honest to everyone at all times. I know Alain de Botton would disagree with this point, and argue a certain amount of dishonesty protects people from hurt. But I say this is a false protection that serves no one. For instance, you may live in a glass house, and feel that you're protected, because those closest to you tell you so. But it's not a real protection if it can shatter in an instant. And yes, any and everything can shatter in an instant. That's life. But, we don't delude ourselves into thinking we'll live forever. Because we understand that's not a protection from our mortality. It's best to be honest so people can formulate their own protections, and make informed choices. With that said, I look forward to Alain's counterargument. As I am someone who can be swayed. (Play-off music) Remember, every great story needs a witness. A witness is different than an audience. A witness is there as it's happening. The burden is then the witness' to relay the story to an audience. (Play-off music intensifies) A great writer makes an audience feel like a witness. The best stories inspire or elevate all audience members to witnesses. That's when they spread like wildfire. God bless great stories, god bless writing, the process, and above all, god bless writers! (Applause)

(Later that night in a hotel room)

**SELENE:** There's something I want to tell you.

**ADONIS:** I don't want to know.

**SELENE:** But you said...

**ADONIS:** Timing is still important. Tell me tomorrow morning. Let us have tonight.


(P.S. If an open relationship then a Sailor Moon wedding then a meteor shower on the beach in the rain)

# Shark (Baby) vs. Bear (Daddy)

1.

Sleeping with a sugar baby is like swimming with the sharks

Being overly generous with a sugar baby is like putting on a seal suit to swim with the sharks

Being a guarantor for a sugar baby is like being nibbled on a little bit at a time in a water tank of piranha

You might survive swimming with sharks—
You might even survive swimming with the sharks in a seal suit—
But there's no way you're surviving a water tank of piranha with all your parts

(P.S. It means in the apartment of the present saga there was a fraud carried out by Selene against all daddies)

2.

Sleeping with a sugar daddy is like poking the bear

Being overly indulgent with a sugar daddy is like feeding the bear

Being a fraud for a sugar daddy is like being locked out with the hyenas for the night

You might survive poking the bear—
You might even survive feeding the bear—
But there's no way you're surviving a pack of howling hyenas smelling like sugar

(P.S. It means breakup by eviction is unavoidable)

# THE NEXT MORNING

**Ain't that Peculiar | Marvin Gaye**

: I act on every temptation.

: Me too.

: It's a spider's web.

: Or—

: Or it's a sail.

: That'll take you on many journeys.

: Some shipwrecks.

: Some utopias, too.

: Always fleeting though.

: That's ok.

: No, it's not. I need forever.

: Forever is the horizon. It's there for the taking.

: I'm lazy.

: I want my own apartment.

: No one else has keys to.

: There's always a safe.

: Did you read my journal?

: Did you want me to?

: It was my journal.

: Not a safe. You knew how I'd react.

: (Laughing) What took you so long?

: You could've just said.

: It was an experiment.

: Now you're being cruel.

: I was afraid. The punishment I imagined...

: I was ignorant of your depths. But you knew mine.

: Not really.

: You knew I'd never hurt you.

: But I deserved it.

: What's the point?

: All's fair in love and war.

: Which is it?

: A question of extremes.

: A question of endurance.

: A scorned lover is collateral damage.

: The one who scorches though—

: They're God!

: God of scorched earth.

: I liked you better when you brought gifts.

: That was our golden era.

: We were good for a time.

: Why'd we stop fucking?

: I wanted bigger gifts.

: I brought bigger gifts.

: I know. I wanted bigger.

: I see.

: I'm there.

: And afterwards?

: Afterwards?

: Afterwards...

: I'm not going to call.

: I believe you this time.

: (Internally) What upsets me is having been so sublime last night.

: (Internally) I knew I was inflating myself with egoism.

(The morning fog dissipates)

: I knew once you saw the real me you'd leave.

: That's not true.

: It is. You saw me. Then you left.

: I saw you. But you kept denying what I saw.

: Hmph!

: I left because you didn't let me in.

: Why would you love me?

: I saw myself in you.

: Huh, so, then I'll be ok.

: Do you think I'm ok?

: You're more ok than me.

: So, then you'll be more ok than you are right now.

(P.S. Everything you wanted yes except you wanted it by magic not by romance)

# AFTERMATH

## *(Hereafter)*

| After Laughter (Comes Tears) | Wendy Rene |

**MÔMO :**

Or, je le répète, le Bardo c'est la mort, **et la mort n'est qu'un état de magie noire qui n'existait pas il n'y a pas si longtemps.**

# (Paradox) Of Love

**Love Is… POISON GiRL FRiEND**

Love's not a feeling.
It's more a dance.
If you cast off your partner,
dance solo, that's not
love. Maybe self-love, but
not love in sense
you share it, experience
it with a partner.
And, if you just
follow your partner's lead
whole time, you're just
being dragged around like
an anchor. Not love!
Love's back and forth
between two people dancing—
pulling, tugging, submitting, going
with flow, but also
surprising other, not being
predictable, not being refined
or boxed into same
dance, song. Love's precarious,
and 50% out of
your control! Also, if
love's dance, it's not
the partner— the partner
can be switched out
indefinitely, cyclically. For those
who prefer control, that's
truly frightening.

(P.S. He who loves Selene is the most charmed lover in the world)

# IMPROMPTU EULOGY (GOD'S SKIT)

**Separate Ways (Worlds Apart) | Journey**

**GOD:**

Shout-out to Adonis, aka Captain Save-a-Hoe. He recently had his heart broken, I mean shredded, just shredded. But he's going to be ok. Because hearts are like lizards, they grow back, bigger, better, stronger. How about a round of applause for his future heart?

(Applause)

Every man goes through a Save-a-Hoe phase at some point in his life, usually in his thirties, when he wants to play the hero, you know, a knight in shining armor. He convinces himself he can do what no other man can, and not only that, that he must do it, that it's his destiny to save that hoe.

(Tittering)

Meanwhile, every woman goes through a Hoe phase at some point in her life, usually in her twenties, when she becomes a hoe to feel that power over men. You know, that power. The power of pussy. The power of sexual compliance. The power of theater, puppet theater. Because a woman in her Hoe phase is the Puppet Master!

(Hooting)

There's no doubt about it. She's pulling all the strings. And all the strings are tied to men's cocks. But men don't see it that way—to great peril! Not during their Save-a-Hoe phase. All they see is a damsel in distress, and an opportunity to prove themselves above other quote-unquote lesser men. But a woman in her Hoe phase does not want to be saved. She does not want a man.

(Women nodding)

Not yet, that is. Because her Trap-a-Man phase doesn't come until after her Hoe phase ends, usually in her thirties, after a decade of hoeing it up, a woman realizes she can't be a hoe forever, so she transitions from Hoe phase to Trap-a-Man phase.

(Men nodding)

The irony here is a woman's Trap-a-Man phase aligns perfectly with a man's Save-a-Hoe phase, and in all likelihood would result in pregnancy, marriage, happily ever after. But here's the rub, as a woman transitions from her Hoe phase to her Trap-a-Man phase, a man transitions from his Save-a-Hoe phase to his Fuck-that-Hoe phase.

(Stomping)

Usually in his forties, after a series of heartbreaks, or one epic heartbreak, as in the case of Adonis, he no longer believes a woman can devote herself to any man, or that any woman is worth his devotion. So, just as a woman enters her Trap-a-Man phase, a man enters his Fuck-that-Hoe phase, destroying any possibility of a genuine connection.

(Gasping)

You see, for both men and women alike, the trick is to recognize what phase the other is in. A woman in her Trap-a-Man phase pairs well with a man in his Save-a-Hoe phase. Likewise, a woman in her Hoe phase pairs well with a man in his Fuck-that-Hoe phase. But any other cross-pairing will result in nuclear destruction for all!

(Applause)

(Improvising) How many hoes you know in their fifties? Maybe some men out there are raging against the dying of the light. But hoes don't want to be hoes forever. Hoeing takes a toll. (Hand on chest) Hoeing takes a toll. (Hand on cock)

(P.S. A cormorant is ruled by an angler or its appetite)

# An Explanation of the Truth

Either Selene is not honest
Or Adonis has a false sense of Selene
And he wants to preserve it

Those who lie, lie off the truth
Veering just slightly

Those who love, see love in every gesture
Veering wildly from the obvious

In certain contexts, the truth can be a lie too
There's nothing like marriage
For mystifying truth

For caging truth inside a lie
The lie of monogamy

Once one has gone through black magic
And climbs out of the spell jar
He is no longer blind

He is traumatized

Not from what he saw
But from what he sees now
In deep contrast with all he held to be true

The explanation is that Adonis
One spring day
(Having found her journal)

Stopped
The fantasy of Selene

Two doors
Within a mile
Were open to him

That of home
That of the apartment
And it was not an easy choice

If he chose home
She would win
In turning him into Daisy

If he chose the apartment
He would no doubt
End up like Gatsby

He always felt Gatsby was his truer destiny
And now more than ever
He felt like he deserved it

        Selene will read this
        And her takeaway will be:
        Stop keeping a journal

        Adonis will read this
        And his takeaway will be:
        I'm tired of Gatsby, *maybe*

        And each in the same way
        Is fatally flawed

        Yet fascinated by their flaws
        Because each in their reflection

        Is their own best audience
        *'So what if no one else claps for me!'*

(P.S. No one else claps)

# CACA

São Paulo | The Weeknd, Anitta

(Roarings here)

**ADONIS:**   As for me, I love nothing but pussy.
I mean pungent pussy, voodoo pussy, per se.
Afterwards:
Black magic,

Black magic afterwards.
First let's make a baby, sans magic.
Later on we'll smoke the pipe of black magic.
Now let's get the baby in your belly, sighing.

Along with magic.
For whatever's been made with magic,
We've made a martyr of.
And where do you think birth control comes from?

That charged confession of a misuse of magic.
And where do you think certain perversions come from?

(P.S. Et le surnaturel, depuis que j'ai été là-haut, ne m'apparaît plus comme quelque chose de si extraordinaire que je ne puisse dire que j'ai été, au sens littéral du terme: *ensorcelé*.)

# Bona Fide Witch

**ALPHAPUSSY | Pixel Grip**

Don't pretend you're good
Don't pretend you're
Don't don't
Don't pretend
You're good
Don't
Your pussy voodoo
My cock go-go
My cock mood
Your pussy rogue
My cock curve
Your pussy don't
Your pussy don't afford
My cock reward
Your pussy voodoo
My cock go-go
My cock mood
Your pussy rogue
My cock curve
Your pussy don't
The gloss off
Bona fide
The act don't start
Til I walk in the door
Don't pretend you're good
Don't pretend you're
Don't don't
Don't pretend
You're good
Don't

(P.S. Don't let the babyface fool you)

# POST SCRIPTUM

Decency | Balthazar

: You're crying, darling.

: I'm not crying.

: What's wrong?

: I've been recast to impose a new decency.

: What's wrong with decency?

: If I spell it out anymore, it's not poetry.

: If you don't, it's ambiguous.

: What makes it poetry is the ambiguity.

: What's the point of communicating then?

: Within the ambiguity, one can illuminate unexpected truths.

: You mean, delusion?

: No!

: If there's delusion, it begins before the source.

: The end is to illuminate the emotion from the inside, anything else is mere description.

: I prefer mere description.

: Darling, you're a slow learner.

: Darling, you're a poor teacher.

: In the copy for the book, I clearly state Adonis is married.

: Where's his wife in the book?

: She's inferred.

: Convenient.

: Protective.

: Please.

: She exists outside fiction, a faithful woman.

(P.S. If the cheetah is eating the cormorant then the cormorant is eating the cheetah then on the beach walks the unicorn)

# Cold Plunge

*Cormorant Bird* | Fionn Regan

I walk into the ocean
without breaking rhythm

despite the cold water
despite the waves

I dolphin dive past the breakers
into a vast deepness

I control my breath (floating
to reset) then I find my stroke

my most poetic gesture
I swim parallel to the shore

most days (feeding an illusion
I could be saved) but not today

today I divorce all my attachments
today I drown my fear

the sun's glare warms me
points me to the horizon

today the horizon seems reachable
today I inhabit my spirit animal

the cormorant
not as taker of corpses

or thief of hearts
but as prince of vampires

ambassador of freaks
negotiating two worlds

within a threshold
a cosmic doorframe

I hover there
I thrive there

I fly and swim
but I cannot fly too high

I cannot breathe underwater
I'm given just enough rope

to hang myself
or lasso a lover

I yearn to see beyond
I yearn to arrive

I understand nothing
of the ocean floor

I cannot decide if it's hunting me
or if I'm hunting an alien love

I'm shocked anyone can love me
stay in love with me

my head heart and cock
are disproportionally large

I wanted to die in your arms
I wanted it literally

you gave it to me
(you let me have it, alright) figuratively

forcing me to recover from it
blood on your hands (holding

a starfish) I have it
the trauma

I'm within its ebbs and flows
(desire) a surfer in a wave

Voila! I emerge exhausted
ebullient I emerged at all

stil seeking your affirmation
but you've already left

I'm crushed by the wave
a world above and below

I see the above (blue-grey sky)
held up by the horizon

below I can't measure distance
I underestimate depth

I misinterpret slants of light
as sharks or stingrays

another picture is forming
on the ocean floor (The Hydra)

I see its many necks and faces
the rest is embedded in the sand

but I recognize it as parent
I'm neither hunter or hunted

all that remains is a vague feeling
that I'm protected (somehow special—

another illusion) and the words
fluorescent in my brain

YOU WILL NOT DIE HERE
I WILL NOT LEAVE YOU

it's hard to accept one's own
demise as it's happening

| | | |
|---|---|---|
| romance | | black magic |
| home | **ocean** | apartment |
| unicorn | | cheetah |

(P.S. The ocean renews you until it takes you)

# CAT'S EYE NEBULA

**A Soulmate Who Wasn't Meant to Be** | Jess Benko

: I upended my life.

: I know

: I regret moving in.

: That hurts.

: Me too.

: You weren't there when I needed you.

: I couldn't stay when I knew you were lying.

: You have too much baggage.

: You have baggage too.

: What do you mean?

: Your malaise.

: You misunderstood.

: You misled.

: We couldn't do what we wanted.

: No, that's not it.

: It is.

: No. Your intentions were nefarious.

: (Crying)

: The way you curate is savage. The way you gaslight is next level.

: All the lies are shameful truths.

: I crave emotional connection.

: I feign emotion.

: That's why we're breaking up.

: Because you don't believe me.

: That's true.

: (Packing) I hate you.

: I thought you could love me.

: (Internally) I did.

: We could've had an open relationship.

(P.S. If I hate you then I love you then I have blood on my hands)

# Little by Little

*Tears* | John Summit, Paige Cavell

To speak of childhood or confess secret lovers
Is a distortion I'm not my childhood nor my secrets

I veered off course in most rewarding way
I treat love as rhizome I have been honest

With you where I have not with others
Without fear of shame or judgment

This has been both liberating and exhilarating
But I have not given enough thought

To mine honesty's effects on you
I need to consider circumstance and context

Outside my own I don't want this to sound
Like an apology because I don't want this to be

An apology I have written love poems to you
I have built a parallel world around you

I have visited you and I have been stirred by your visits
However infrequent they are they are how I tell the truth

(P.S. I step into the moonlight)

# Side by Side

*Translation | Swim Team, Rebecca Brunner, Delance*

We peek in on each other through our poetry
And the poetry of friends what I glimpse

I devour what I offer for view I hope
Is desirable something close to your beauty

Intelligence to warrant your attention
I find myself speaking in a new voice

But my naiveté remains a lapse in convention
Please don't perceive it as betrayal

What offsets my lack is my curiosity
I want to learn your mode of artmaking

How you curate your image off the page
To read what you read to absorb your voice

In your audience I feel heard and seen
Lifted up by your discretion




(P.S. I step out of the moonlight)

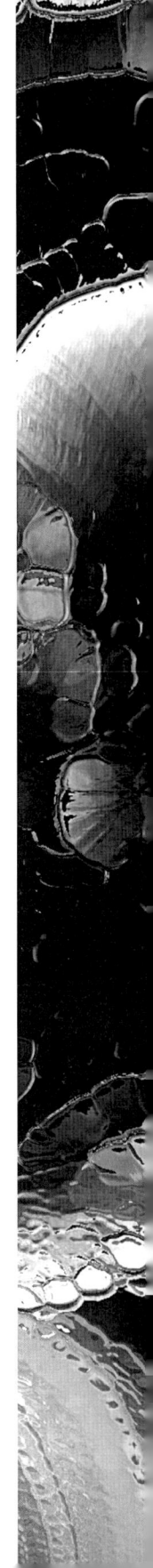

# AFTER SPICER (A SÉANCE)

**All Is Soft Inside | AURORA**

1. 1A (A Translation for Andrew Levy)

A cormorant
Is there
At the center of the apartment or the cosmos or my mouth
And there is nothing in the saga like cormorant
Nothing in the deviant city

The afterlife is a cheetah resting on a chair at the end of the bar

A man grunts at the apartment
A man grunts at the cosmos
A man grunts at the mouth
A man grunts with radiant city

I ask for the afterlife to be as radiant as a cheetah's skin

The saga falls apart and spawns a cormorant
Two faces called cheetah are gracefully walking out where the stage is
The man is alone there with the apartment, with the cosmos, with my mouth
And there is nothing in the saga like cormorant
Nothing in the deviant city

(P.S. Black magic took from me all I had)

2. Rapid Passage (A Translation for 'I Shall Never Name')

A friend
Who I shall never see
Has blocked me on her phone
A friend
Who I shall never see—

Along the coast
There's a highway
And the cars speed
With high beams into glass houses

In the past I undressed
The friend
Who I shall never see

A friend ashamed of me
And my kink

A friend ashamed of secret
Trysts in cheap hotels

A friend of Veil Nebula that's drifting
Along flashing lights

(P.S. The love that was already in me)

3. Siren (A Translation for Selene)

Her black magic
In her smoke paraphernalia for the bedroom
Naked for her virtual lovers and Adonis
Curates poses as Lolita

Her audience stays awake
Hot for hearts and kisses
She puts on makeup for her profile
Scrolling through the entire night of always

Her black magic
Was eating her from the inside
In her need for control
She lost the freedom to disappear or start over

(P.S. I suffered long enough I reasoned to deserve voodoo pussy)

4. Sosúa (A Translation for Kilroy)

Her baggage at afterlife of Playa Alicia.

> — It is sunrise. A dead stingray
> Has washed up on the beach.
> Some white clouds
> And a cheetah.

Her hotel at afterlife of Playa Alicia.

> — Her son is with her grandmother.
> Large waves pound the shore.
> I am inside at the bar
> Wearing linen shorts the color of my skin.
> At sunrise
> Some empty bottles
> And a cheetah.

Afterlife at the bar,
¿Por qué ladra un perro?

> — It is sunrise
> Some buried corpses
> And a cheetah.

(P.S. And now I walk on the beach protector of the unicorn)

## An Embodied Experience

*Can't Go Wrong Without You | His Name is Alive*

Adonis misunderstood "the relationship,"
Selene points out.

The error causes him to fly and swim.
He gorges on his delusion.

He realizes Selene is at home,
Too at home in trauma and deceit.

She wants to control him.
She reasons this is fair BECAUSE of her trauma.

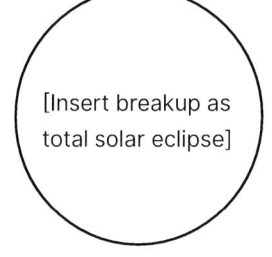

[Insert breakup as total solar eclipse]

Adonis blooms after Selene.
But he never regains his mania.

He experiences this as a great loss
To his erections. (Hand cradles cock)

(P.S. When I believed I was falling in love I know now I was falling under a spell)

# Rhizome (Ballad of Escape)

|  | (upward) | (up) | (multi- | (linear) |  |
|---|---|---|---|---|---|
| escape hatch | escape pod | fire escape | narrow escape | escape plan | escape artist |
| (downward) |  | (down) | -dimensional) |  | (omnipresent) |

*I Will Run from You | Cemeteries*

**ENZO:** A con artist starts by picking the right mark.

**ROACH:** To not be seen. Because to be seen is to be smooshed.

**RICH MAN:** Do you know the phrase 'hedging your bets?' That's Selene.

**BARTENDER:** Walking, sitting, standing, and lying down are the four postures of Zen meditation. Adonis added to that swimming, and fucking.

The greatest con is when the mark, recognizing the con, flips the script.

Wenn der Reiter nichts taugt,
ist das Pferd schuld.

Adonis is anyone who escapes. But no one escapes intact.

(P.S. She wasn't hedging her bets. She was keeping a reserve supply.)

# (Tinnitus) NOISE OF SOSUA

Yo Miss | Luis Brown

# Balcony

*Bongos | Cardi B, Megan Thee Stallion*

Except for the wet bathing suit hanging,
Except for his wet hair, which he keeps untied,
Except for his chest, which feels waterlogged,

Adonis has everything dry—

He has a method to dry himself
By simply undressing,
Spreading limbs—

If only lighting incense
Could turn down volume of dusk—

He stays naked in the dark:

Dogs barking,
Cheetahs outside the gate,
Alicorn of the unicorn in the trees.

(P.S. Light knocking on door)

# A GREAT CRY

*Rim* | Brook Candy, Aquaria, Violet Chachki

**ADONIS:** My sexual life is completely shot through with S&M and unhygienic gymnastics that are expressed in semen and bodily fluids. And my kinks are of a more troubling matter. They are themselves taboo and ill-advised. They have traumatic roots, roots of trauma that reach back to the beginning of life. But they have not the bliss of life. One does not feel in them satisfaction or content no matter the carnal conquests. They are the afflictions of a mind that does not ponder consequences. If it had, it would render those consequences a sufficient deterrent. And there lies the entire problem: to have within oneself the manic desire and physical dexterity of a taut cock to such a degree of tautness that it cannot but explode, to have an abundance of partners and actresses for hire who might join in the performance, might feed their own purpose. And at the very moment when the inner voice, the ego, is about to confess guilt, shame, self-doubt, at that dangerous moment when the performance is threatened, a higher and more potent inner voice, the super ego, murders the self-doubt, murders the shame, murders the guilt and leaves me panting at the altar of the feminine asshole.

(P.S. You have to eat ass, just once)

100

## (Barking)

*I Wanna Be Your Dog | Mephisto Walz*

With me in my pants
There is a dog
A dog in my pants
There is no muzzling it
It barks

It is the smell of ass crack

Oh Sinbad
Quit your barking

(P.S. Quit your sniffing)

# (Dying)

*Sperm Like Honey | The frozen Autumn*

It was the sildenafil, after all
That let him down.

So, he went night swimming
Under a full moon,
Nude:

At least this is glorious.
It could have been me passing out
At Captain Bailee's.

(P.S. Gringo se desmaya en un bar - TikTok video)

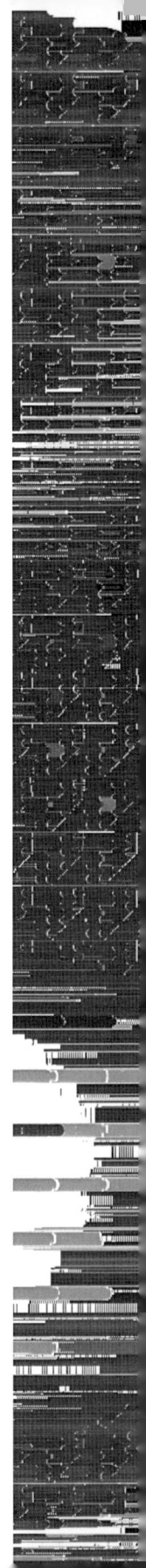

# HAPPY VALENTINE'S DAY XOXOXO
*The Perfect Girl - Soft Kill Remix* | Mareux, Soft Kill

**MONSIEUR:** J'aime et j'affirme comme une valentine chaque femme soi-disant dépravée.

**ADONIS:** I love and affirm as a valentine every woman most willing to perform anal sex.

**MONSIEUR:** Je préfère baiser plutôt que de me sentir idolâtré.

**ADONIS:** I love and affirm as a valentine every woman who confesses to an abortion, who does not wish to clone herself.

**MONSIEUR:** J'aime et j'affirme comme une valentine toute femme qui nourrit entièrement ses désirs, et qui se délecte de l'image d'une chatte poilue.

**ADONIS:** I don't have a condom. I love and affirm as a valentine every woman who poisons herself without having an antidote.

**MONSIEUR:** J'aime et j'affirme comme une valentine chaque femme qui refuse le maquillage parce qu'il défigure sa beauté.

**ADONIS:** I love and affirm as a valentine every woman who considers her asshole the navel of her womanhood, and a door to the cosmos.

**MONSIEUR:** J'aime et j'affirme comme une valentine chaque femme qui ruine sa carrière en dansante dans une afterparty ou une discothèque.

**ADONIS:** I love and affirm as a valentine every woman who consorts with characters of ill repute to enhance her powers of divination.

**MONSIEUR:** J'aime et j'affirme comme une valentine chaque femme qui se soumet à la luxure, à l'éros et à la subjugation de son clitoris.

**ADONIS:** I love and affirm as a valentine every woman who agrees to any roleplay whatsoever beyond the limits of her apprehension.

**MONSIEUR:** J'aime et j'affirme comme une valentine chaque femme qui se désigne comme un agent de magie noire, une sorcière ou un guépard.

**ADONIS:** I love and affirm as a valentine every woman who finishes acrobatically, or comfortably, in the ass.

**MONSIEUR:** J'aime et j'affirme comme une valentine chaque femme dont la chatte pue comme elle sent douce, et sent encore plus bon quand elle pue vraiment, c'est-à-dire quand elle transpire.

**ADONIS:** I love and affirm as a valentine every woman who suffers 200 failed attempts in the ass until she finally orgasms.

**MONSIEUR:** J'aime et j'affirme comme une valentine chaque femme qui définit son caractère comme étant à la recherche d'une vie sans maquillage.

**ADONIS:** I love and affirm as a valentine every woman most willing to sustain 200 failed attempts in the ass to promote the anal orgasm.

**MONSIEUR:** J'aime et j'affirme comme une valentine chaque femme qui évite le miroir, sauf lorsqu'elle est pénétrée par derrière.

**ADONIS:** I love and affirm as a valentine every woman who gives herself over to the depravities of porn without first having tested them.

**MONSIEUR:** J'aime et j'affirme comme une valentine chaque femme qui poursuit pour elle-même la dégradation de sa chatte.

**ADONIS:** I love and affirm as a valentine every woman who rejects dignity in pursuit of sexual gymnastics.

**MONSIEUR:** J'aime et j'affirme comme une valentine chaque femme qui ne se considère rien de plus qu'une chatte maudite à pratiquer le sexe anal sous l'angle de la cowgirl inversée.

**ADONIS:** I love and affirm as a valentine every woman who can endure anal sex on a full bladder to coincide her orgasm with urination.

**MONSIEUR:** J'aime et j'affirme comme une valentine chaque femme qui définit son rôle comme une performance pour sa damnation.

**ADONIS:** I love and affirm as a valentine every woman who cuddles right away after being ravished, i.e. sticky and stinking.

**MONSIEUR:** J'aime, avant tout, et j'affirme comme une valentine chaque femme la plus disposée à ajouter des bâillonnements et des larmes à sa performance.

**ADONIS:** After all, I love and affirm as a valentine every woman who concedes her pussy is irredeemable.

**MONSIEUR:** Pour conclure, la seule chatte rachetable est le cul, c'est-à-dire la mine d'or de CACA.

**ADONIS:** I am captain-save-a-ho, daddy, and unholy. I idolize no pussy. I love and affirm the feminine asshole.

**MONSIEUR:** J'ai de la virilité parce que j'ai de la virilité, j'aime et j'affirme comme une valentine toute femme qui veut que je le prouve.

**ADONIS:** I love and affirm as a valentine every soi-disant depraved woman.

**MONSIEUR:** J'aime et j'affirme la nature sauvage de chaque femme.

**ADONIS:** I am by nature obscene, mature. Obscenely mature.

**MONSIEUR:** J'aime et j'affirme toute dépravation que l'on pourrait souhaiter reproduire dans une performance.

**ADONIS:** I came to Sosúa to make peace with voodoo pussy. You invented this language, not me.

**MONSIEUR:** Nous ne parlons pas encore couramment.

**ADONIS:** We are 'Not the World.'

**MONSIEUR:** Il n'y a pas de glaçage sur le gâteau.

**ADONIS:** The scene has not been rehearsed. The crème de la crème not yet arrived at.

**MONSIEUR:** La seule controverse est celle d'avoir une chatte ou une bite, et CACA suffit à renforcer sa libido contre les normes prudes.

**ADONIS:** I do not censor myself. I do not promise or threaten. I am unpredictable because I am open-minded.

**MONSIEUR:** Tu es venu à Sosua pour faire la paix avec la chatte vaudou.

**ADONIS:** But I blacked out in a crowded bar and I woke up on my side. There remains to be solved the mystery of how I hit the floor, if a spell was cast on me, a spell of black magic.

**MONSIEUR:** Je n'idolâtrerai aucune chatte. Mais pour le trou du cul féminin, je viderai mon ventre de lait, d'élan vital, de joie de vivre.

(P.S. Nothing can be explained except by the compulsions of the libido)

## Of Spiders

*Fatal Attraction* | Reed Wonder, Aurora Olivas

The cock
Spills its milk

Perhaps you'll find a pussy
I won't say putrid
But with a huge clitoris

A pussy, I said
But of that pussy
I cannot predict its potency

From its aperture
The black widow eats her lover

(P.S. That is, *sometimes* eats her lover)

# Lost and Found (Art of Self-Portraiture)

El Muchacho de los Ojos Tristes | Jeanette

Where is my Valentine?
Who sleeps folded next to me

like an accordion? Who leaves in the morning
like a lung emptied? Not a great cry.

Not even a giant sneeze.
But a desperate sigh.

Who sees me in the mirror
nude, yearning to be drawn?

Whoever judges me as exhibitionist
has already lost my art.

I am both hand and eye,
tracing my lines with a finger

before mixing egg with paint.
I bring my finger to my face

and inhale my scent. When I exhale
I pour myself on canvas.

(P.S. Leche de Adonis)

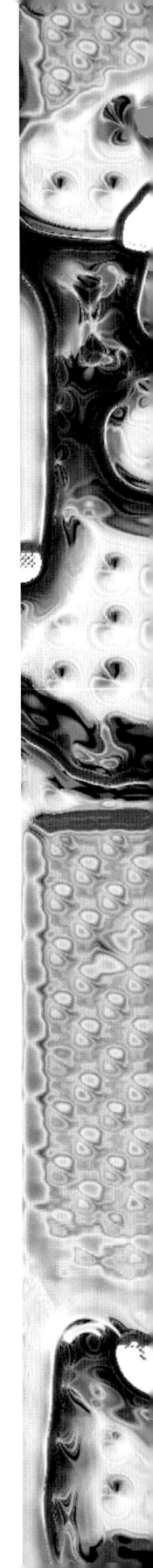

# FANTASTICAL LIARS
**No Alibis | Eric Clapton**

**ADONIS:** I attract the most fantastical liars. My dad was first and foremost. I had a girlfriend who was next level. And recently, I met Carmine in a bar. There must be something about me. I must have the face of an audience.

**MONSIEUR:** Un public naïf.

**ADONIS:** With all of them, I started out genuinely believing them. My dad for years, my girlfriend for months, and Carmine for the first few minutes. I don't know…

**MONSIEUR:** Tu tombes dedans.

**ADONIS:** I fall in…

**MONSIEUR:** Tu es un imbécile.

**ADONIS:** But I'm getting better at seeing through the lies.

**MONSIEUR:** Comment mesurer l'amélioration?

**ADONIS:** When I believe them, I write a certain poetry. When I stop believing them, I write another type of poetry. When I compare these two types of poetry, I realize, I too—

**MONSIEUR:** Peut-être plus—

**ADONIS:** Am a fantastical liar!

**MONSIEUR:** Dis-moi encore une fois, pourquoi es-tu venu à Sosua?

**ADONIS:** To marry Chanty.

**MONSIEUR:** Où est-elle?

**ADONIS:** Or to die.

**MONSIEUR:** Un lâche meurt mille fois.

(P.S. Every lie is a dagger)

# An Opera (Pyre)

*Fire in These Hills* | Imagine Dragons

I write my life in dialogue,
and inside the dialogue
I write
*Green Of Each Window*. "Ah me."

I write *Crystalline Green*,
that is after,
somewhere between innocence
and experience. "Oh Selene!"

I write *Afterwards*
in dialogue,
direct and unapologetic,
with the clarity of a defeated man. "And then."

(P.S. A ship burial)

# Desperation in Adonis

*Let Me Live/Let Me Die* | *Des Rocs*

What makes desperate so desperate?
Desperate soul, desperate man,
Desperate husband, desperate dog,
Desperate cock, desperate sex.
So much desperation in Adonis.
Dean, Decatur, Degraw,
Dekalb... Desperate boulevard,
Desperate city, desperate state.
But what if, like James Bond,
The hero comes out on top? Is it
The epitome of confident,
Or a byproduct of grave fiction?

(P.S. What of the antihero?)

# ALONE IN CHANTY'S APARTMENT
*Hideaway* | Kiesza

(Quietly staring in dresser mirror)

**ADONIS:** Who are you?

(Quietly staring)

**ADONIS:** More importantly, what do you want?

(Quietly staring)

**ADONIS:** (Grunting)

(He goes to bathroom)

**ADONIS:** (On toilet) I'm ready to be kicked out. I'm ready to stay. That's the problem, I'm waiting for someone to decide.

(He turns on shower, which requires filling a bucket and pouring it over himself)

**ADONIS:** (In shower) I realize who I am. I am whoever stands in front of me, shows interest. Or feigns interest...

(P.S. I like being somewhere no one can guess where I am)

# DRAWER
*full of wigs*

## Playa Alicia (Reprise)

*I'm Your Man | Mitski*

I want to walk on the beach
Where the water is calm and clear.

I want to pet the mane of the unicorn
As robust and fine as silk,

Hold it firm as my wife
Till all the past is forgiven.

For the cormorant's grunt is the grittiest.

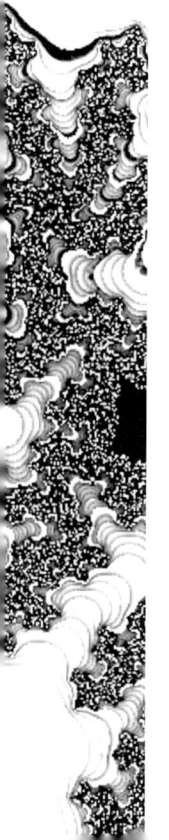

(P.S. Le besoin est tel que l'océan ne peut l'apaiser)

# Going Home

*A thousand years | Christina Perri*

I'll do the housework.
Give me the chemotherapy
From the expensive IV.
I'll digest the premeds.

I'll sell lotto for the poor
And carry the heavy groceries
For the grandmother with four dead sons.
The lump is in your breast, my unicorn.

I'll learn the green cure
From the Chinese herbalist.
I am the cormorant and I'll hunt
To appease your need.

Three children grew in our house.
They played the funny sitcom,
Each with their own personality and a laugh
That was the contagion of our joy.

I walked on the beach where we met,
The dirty sand and notorious beach.
A life was saved as part of a drill.
Let God decide who will drown.

(P.S. I will save you every time)

# (Passport Control) AERODROME

SABINA之淚 | my little airport

# Aerodrome (Arrival)

<small>Paradise City | Guns N' Roses</small>

Monsieur opens the shutters,
"L'homme qui pense se dépense complètement."

This cock evokes CACA
and the Afterlife, the apartment,
the beach, the bedroom.
The marrow of the cock
seems to be silk
or nylon or rope, but
taut rope. An inch
is therefore an eternity. And
the grunt of the
cormorant a great cry, sonorous
and desperate, in an
eternity collar. The sky changes
colors in eternity, halos,
sun dogs, light pillars. Passport
to eternity is through
pelvic floor. Eternity does, conveniently,
have its runway near
the city. It is the
landscape of a certain
root which never stops burrowing.
The commotion it gives
is that of 'lavish edging.'

"Quant à moi, je
 suis venu faire la paix."


(P.S. Welcome to Sosúa))

# A REAL TRAGEDY
**Can't Pretend | Tom Odell**

(Airport Bar)

**ADONIS:** The sirens were muted.

**BARTENDER:** A complete silence?

**ADONIS:** Yes, but at the shoreline— (Quivers)

**BARTENDER:** What do you mean?

**ADONIS:** A giant wave.

**BARTENDER:** When?

**ADONIS:** Noon.

**BARTENDER:** And then?

**ADONIS:** (Engine roaring) The sky.

**BARTENDER:** How could it have happened?

**ADONIS:** A real tragedy.

**BARTENDER:** But he?

**ADONIS:** He entered the ambulance.

**BARTENDER:** His neck?

**ADONIS:** Broken.

**BARTENDER:** Was he already dead?

**ADONIS:** Yes, but he pretended not.

**BARTENDER:** And the sky?

**ADONIS:** The sky was blue, sky-blue.

**BARTENDER:** He died behind the restaurant?

**ADONIS:** No, beyond the horizon. A few meters beyond.

**BARTENDER:** How do you know?

**ADONIS:** I saw him.

**BARTENDER:** He definitely broke his neck?

**ADONIS:** Yes.

**BARTENDER:** But he swore he was ok.

**ADONIS:** Yes, he told everyone he was ok.

(P.S. I guess that's love)

# Myth of the Two Brothers

Did someone say
What's he doing there
Lying in the sand?

A young old man of fifty
Why did you go to Sosúa?
What did they say, the sirens?

That you were too old
Or just right?
Maybe a little too direct

Did you hit your head
When you passed out at Bailee's?
Oh, how is your knee now?

The US dollar is down
The price for love is up
Compared to a year ago

Did you tell them
I'll find love elsewhere
What's love got to do with it?

That's my karaoke song
That and you say he's just a friend
I'm not in the mood to sing

Why do I keep coming here?
My brother wants to know
But then cuts me off

Actually, I don't want to know!
His cage is made of twigs
He calls it home

When we were boys
We'd fight all the time
They called us the destroyers

One time he pulled a steak knife on me
Another time he threw a billiard ball
It missed me but hit our cousin

In one game, one of us would play dead
And try to wiggle off the bed, head-first
The other would try to prevent the fall

We were full of drama then
Too many B movies and soap operas
(Greek mythology of American childhood)

We still carry that drama with us
He edits films
Fixing other peoples' stories

I write poetry
Extracting my story
From other peoples' lives

I wonder
Without the drama
Would he stop my falling?

(P.S. Would I even notice his?)

# THREE GUYS WALK INTO A BAR (SCENE)

**Games Continued - Radio Edit** | **Bakermat, GoldFish, Marie Plassard**

(God's behind the bar)

**BARTENDER:** Seltzer, no lime.

**GOD:** What are you afraid of, having a good time? (Serves him)

**BARTENDER:** No, I work tonight.

**RICH MAN:** Rye, neat.

**GOD:** A real man. (Nods approval)

**RICH MAN:** (Pays) Keep the change.

**GOD:** Thank you. (Serves him)

**ADONIS:** What do you have on tap?

**GOD:** Can't you read?

**ADONIS:** It's in Spanish.

**GOD:** El tonto. (Serves him)

**ADONIS:** What's this?

**GOD:** American Imperial Porter. (Nods approval to Chanty to enter bar)

**ADONIS:** (Sips) Not bad.

**CHANTY:** (To Bartender) What are you drinking?

(P.S. From dusk til doom)

# Chanty Dolarz

**Si Antes Te Hubiera Conocido | KAROL G**

My future wife
Has a machine gun
Tattoo on her neck
A full arm sleeve
Is thirty years younger
And speaks no English
God, I love her so much!

(P.S. She is of the earthly ones)

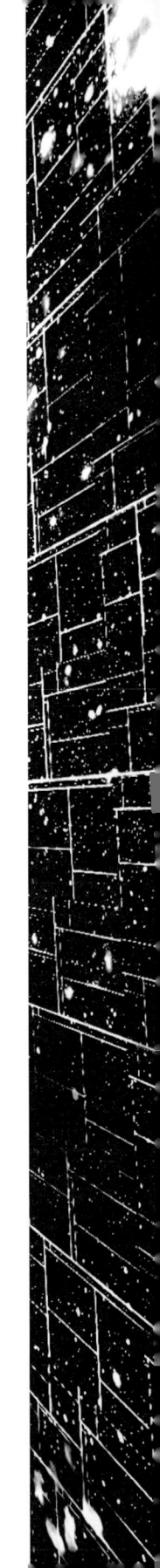

# Complete Playlist of *Afterwards* (Including Interludes) [Title Cards Version]

> Saying goodbye to a ghost is more final than saying goodbye to a lover. Even the dead return, but a ghost, once loved, departing will never reappear. —**Jack Spicer**, *"Dear Lorca,"*

| | | |
|---|---|---|
| After The Storm | Kali Uchis, Tyler, The Creator, Bootsy Collins | 3:27 |
| Gold | Emily Anderson | 3:19 |
| August | Raury, "The Tumultous" Tor. | 3:57 |
| Paint It, Black | The Rolling Stones | 3:22 |
| Mute the Noise | Wiley | 2:49 |
| Time Moves Slow | BADBADNOTGOOD, Samuel T. Herring | 4:34 |
| Explanations | Gil Scott-Heron | 4:12 |
| Infinity | The xx | 5:13 |
| The Gambler | Kenny Rogers | 3:35 |
| Time + Space | Thievery Corporation, Lou Lou Ghelickhani | 4:32 |
| Time Will Tell | Blood Orange | 5:38 |
| Hold you again | The Millenial Club | 3:54 |
| Αθήνα μου | Κωνσταντίνος Αργυρός | 3:49 |
| Deep Forest Green | Husky Rescue | 3:59 |
| God Knows I Tried | Lana Del Rey | 4:40 |
| Andata | Ryuichi Sakamoto | 2:53 |
| Tu dice que tu ta to | Ezzy R, Yoan Retro | 1:51 |
| Ain't Gonna Call | Yellow House | 3:39 |
| Stirb nicht vor mir | Rammstein | 4:05 |
| The Beast In Me | Johnny Cash | 2:45 |
| Galassie | Irama | 3:39 |
| Roi – Instrumental | Mckyyy | 1:23 |
| Cocaine | Dreams We've Had | 6:04 |
| WITHOUT YOU | The Kid LAROI | 2:41 |
| Captain Save A Hoe | E-40, The Click, Suga T, D-Shott, B-Legit | 4:48 |
| Bite The Pillow | ATG Sheed | 2:11 |
| Heavydirtysoul | Twenty One Pilots | 3:54 |

| | | |
|---|---|---|
| *Going Home* | Alice Coltrane | 10:01 |
| *Cherry* | Chromatics | 4:31 |
| *Rump Punch* | Cash Cobain | 2:03 |
| *Nightdrive with You (Fear Of Tigers Remix)* | Anoraak, Fear Of Tigers | 5:55 |
| *Into The Freedom* | Uyama Hiroto | 1:24 |
| *Forget* | Fashion Club, Perfume Genius | 3:26 |
| *Bekle Dedi Gitti – Çizik* | Kaan Tangöze | 4:37 |
| *Take Me To Hell* | Chloe Adams | 2:12 |
| *Lay Back* | CLAVVS | 3:49 |
| *Poly Amor* | Tora | 3:23 |
| *Anything You Want* | Acopia | 3:01 |
| *Lisbon* | Wolf Alice | 3:26 |
| *Aftercare* | Twelve25 | 3:20 |
| *I Can See Clearly Now – Edit* | Johnny Nash | 2:45 |
| *Champagne Room* | Sizzy Rocket | 4:20 |
| *Principles of Lust – The Omen Mix* | Enigma, Sven Väth | 5:51 |
| *It's Complicated* | Sassy 009 | 4:11 |
| *You Don't Need to Sin to Win My Love* | YULLOLA | 2:06 |
| *What Fiction Is For* | DYAN | 4:36 |
| *The Cut That Always Bleeds* | Conan Gray | 3:52 |
| *Beyond Love – Live* | The The | 4:41 |
| *Trap* | SAINt JHN, Lil Baby | 3:05 |
| *Bathroom* | Montell Fish | 3:28 |
| *Bilingual* | Jarina De Marco | 3:23 |
| *Skylark* | Art Blakey | 4:51 |
| *Phoenix* | Anachnid | 1:57 |
| *Never Say Never Again* | Lani Hall | 3:06 |
| *Kill This Love* | BLACKPINK | 3:11 |
| *Ain't That Peculiar* | Marvin Gaye | 2:59 |
| *After Laughter (Comes Tears)* | Wendy Rene | 3:02 |
| *Love Is...* | POiSON GiRL FRiEND | 5:34 |
| *Separate Ways (Worlds Apart)* | Journey | 5:23 |
| *Black Magic* | Jaymes Young | 3:43 |
| *São Paulo* | The Weeknd, Anitta | 5:01 |
| *ALPHAPUSSY* | Pixel Grip | 3:38 |

| | | |
|---|---|---|
| Decency | Balthazar | 4:00 |
| Cormorant Bird | Fionn Regan | 3:27 |
| A Soulmate Who Wasn't Meant to Be | Jess Banko | 5:17 |
| Tears | John Summit, Paige Cavell | 3:56 |
| Translation | Swim Team, Rebecca Brunner, Delance | 4:16 |
| All Is Soft Inside | AURORA | 5:09 |
| Can't Go Wrong Without You | His Name Is Alive | 3:16 |
| I Will Run from You | Cemeteries | 4:29 |
| Yo Miss | Luis Brown | 2:13 |
| Bongos | Cardi B, Megan Thee Stallion | 2:55 |
| Rim | Brooke Candy, Aquaria, Violet Chachki | 3:24 |
| Black Hole Sun | Soundgarden | 5:19 |
| I Wanna Be Your Dog | Mephisto Walz | 4:33 |
| Sperm Like Honey | The frozen Autumn | 3:53 |
| The Perfect Girl – Soft Kill Remix | Mareux, Soft Kill | 3:09 |
| Fatal Attraction | Reed Wonder, Aurora Olivas | 3:23 |
| El Muchacho de los Ojos Tristes | Jeanette | 3:27 |
| No Alibis | Eric Clapton | 5:39 |
| Fire in These Hills | Imagine Dragons | 3:39 |
| Let Me Live / Let Me Die | Des Rocs | 3:27 |
| Hideaway | Kiesza | 4:12 |
| Wigs | City Girls | 2:08 |
| I'm Your Man | Mitski | 3:30 |
| A thousand years | Christina Perri | 4:45 |
| SABINA之淚 | my little airport | 2:20 |
| Paradise City | Guns N' Roses | 6:46 |
| Can't Pretend | Tom Odell | 3:41 |
| Destroyer | TR/ST | 3:12 |
| Games Continued – Radio Edit | Bakermat, GoldFish, Marie Plassard | 3:23 |
| Si Antes Te Hubiera Conocido | KAROL G | 3:16 |
| **Afterlife** | **Hailee Steinfeld** | **3:29** |
| Heaven and Hell | Black Sabbath | 6:59 |

**6h 3m**

# Black Magic Does Exist (Departure)

*Heaven and Hell | Black Sabbath*

There is a certain charm when reality is inverted,
that is, when one reality is inverted alongside all reality,

and steered by witchcraft.
Too often I placed myself on the bow.

But you're all actors.
I mean dogs.

You go around barking, sniffing,
not seeing beyond a few meters.

Faith has to be enough at some point.
As for myself, I'm going home.

I'm done deciphering Selene.
I'm going back to being a man,

not an actor or dog.
Here: take my red nose. No more masks!

(P.S. You are now leaving Sosúa)

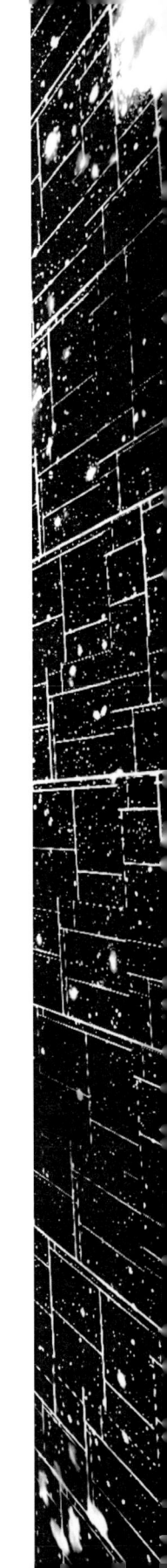